Contents

Magic Belt Series Workbook
for Books 1–12

Name: ______________________________

Students can use this page as a personalized front cover for their work folder.

Introduction to the Magic Belt Series workbook

The Magic Belt reading series and workbook are a reading resource for 'catch up' students age 8–14 who have poor phonic knowledge and would benefit from starting a reading program from the very beginning.

Combined with the reading experience of the Magic Belt Series, the student is engaged and motivated by an exciting quest-like journey throughout his/her progress. The activities in this workbook introduce new knowledge in each chapter, while offering enough practice so that the student is ready to move onto the next level feeling confident and able.

Twelve chapters in this workbook correspond to the reading books in the Magic Belt Series. Each chapter includes activities that develop reading skills: word-building, blending and segmenting words, phoneme manipulation, comprehension, writing and vocabulary work.

The activities are differentiated so that the teacher can choose the appropriate activities for the student. The variety of activities within each chapter offer the teacher choice so that he/she can vary them from lesson to lesson. It is recommended to include word-building and the 'Full circle' game when a new sound or spelling is introduced to make sure the student has internalized the new knowledge before reading the text.

Some activities prepare the student for reading the reading books and should be introduced **before reading the books**, e.g. word-building, phoneme manipulation, caption reading and spelling etc. Other activities **follow the reading of the books,** such as 'Questions for discussion', comprehension and vocabulary activities. As they are based on the stories in the books, the students will need to have read the stories first.

This workbook begins at VCC (vowel/consonant/consonant) and CVCC level. This is a suitable starting point for students who know the sounds of the alphabet and can blend words at CVC level. To see an overview of all four quest series available, see the table on the inside cover of this workbook. The four series can be used for teaching in 'catch-up groups' or with individual students.

Each sheet includes instructions on how to use it with the student.

Some teaching points

The importance of teaching reading and spelling together

In order for the student to understand that spelling (encoding) is the reverse activity of reading (decoding), it important for the student to practice both side by side. For this reason, reading and spelling are taught within word-building, reading and spelling activities and within two-syllable work. Dictation offers the student a 'safe' opportunity to spell selected words correctly. This builds up confidence and develops good spelling strategies.

Pronunciation

Pronunciation of some sounds in words may vary, according to regional accents. The word lists may not always match the pronunciation of the student. This point should be discussed and the lists adapted to the student.

Splitting multisyllabic words

It is important to teach students how to split multisyllabic words. This will enable them to use successful and independent strategies when reading and spelling long words. There are a number of approaches to splitting multisyllabic words depending on the teaching method:

- A spelling-rules approach, e.g. the doubling rule: s i t / t i ng
- A phonic approach which maintains phoneme/grapheme fidelity, e.g. s i tt / i ng
- A morpheme approach which emphasizes the meaning of parts of the word: l i f t /ed

This workbook allows the teacher to use any method he/she is teaching the student.

New vocabulary

Each book in the reading series and the corresponding worksheets introduce new vocabulary. This is an opportunity to learn new vocabulary. The explanation of the words relates to the words as they appear in the text. The teacher may wish to explore additional meanings of the words with the student.

Phonic progression in the Magic Belt Series Books 1–12:

Magic Belt series	Title of book	Phonic progression	Word and text level
Book 1	The Man in the Mist	CVC, VCC and CVCC	CVC, VCC and CVCC
Book 2	Ten Rocks	CVCC	CVCC
Book 3	"Help Us!"	CVCC	CVCC
Book 4	The Clam	CCVC and suffix –ed	CCVC
Book 5	Crabs!	CCVCC	CCVCC
Book 6	Crunch!	spellings <ch> and <tch>*	CCVCC
Book 7	Hush!	'sh' **	CCVCC
Book 8	The Sixth Rock	<th> – two sounds	CCVCC
Book 9	Golem of the Rocks	<ck> and <qu>***	CCVCC
Book 10	Dung!	'ng'	CCVCC
Book 11	The Spitting Pot	<wh> and suffix –ing	CCVCC
Book 12	The Simple Plot	<le>	CCVCC

* < > = a spelling (grapheme), e.g. the <ck> spelling for the sound 'k'

** ' ' = a sound in a word (phoneme), e.g. the sound 'sh'

*** = <qu> spells two sounds ('k' and 'w'). In English, the letter <q> commonly appears with the letter <u> to spell the sound 'kw' (quick, queen, quiet, etc). For convenience sake, they are taught together.

Book 1: The Man in the Mist

Questions for discussion

Chapter 1

1. The word 'kid' can mean two things. What are they? (p. 1)
2. Why can't Grandpa get up? (p. 3)

Chapter 2

1. What does the word 'kin' mean? (p. 4)
2. What is a 'nag' in the story? (p. 5)
3. What does Zak decide to do? (p. 5)

Chapter 3

1. Who does Zak see in the fog? (p. 7)
2. What is the man wearing? (p. 8)

Chapter 4

1. What is different about the man's belt? (p. 10)
2. What does the man have on his lap? (p. 11)
3. How do you think Zak feels when he lets the man ride in his wagon? (p. 12)

Teaching guidelines:
These questions can be discussed after reading the text. They will help develop speaking and listening skills, comprehension and vocabulary.

Book 1: Word-building VCC words

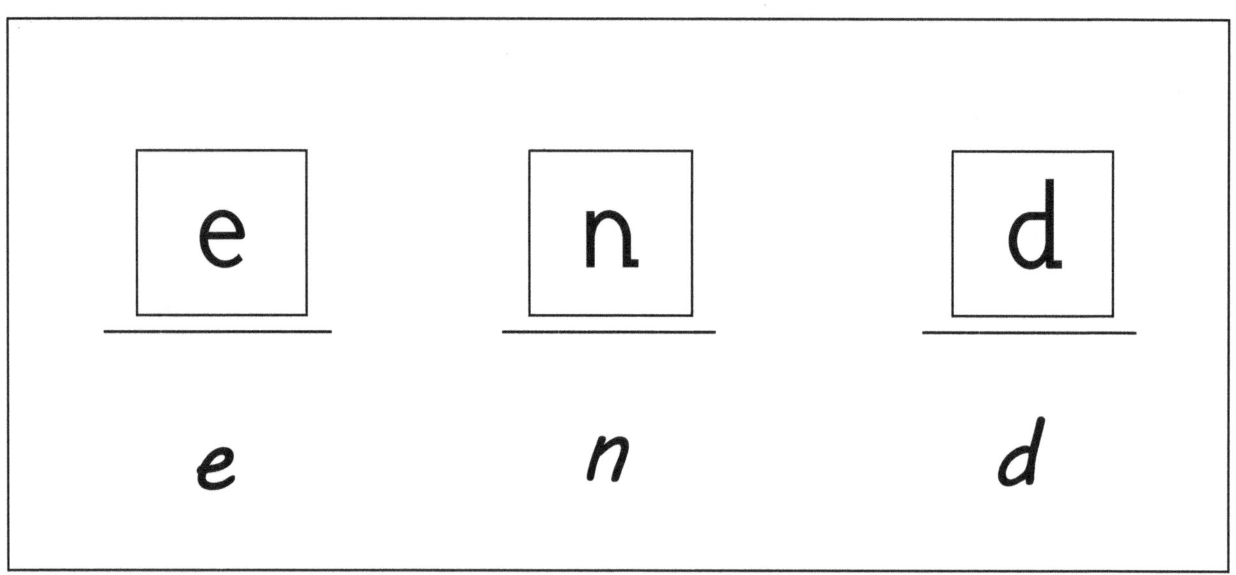

Teaching aims:

- Segment and blend VCC (vowel/consonant/consonant) words with the sounds of the alphabet.

Teacher guidelines:
Use a white board on which three lines have been drawn. Use the cards from the introductory levels for word-building.

Teach word-building
Select a word from the list below. Use only the letters needed to build that word and jumble them up. Ask the student to build that word by listening to the sounds in the word and segmenting all the sounds in the word, one at a time. The student then places each card on the appropriate line once he/she has segmented the word. Ask the student to read the word he/she has built. Ask the student to write the word under the lines, saying the sounds as he/she does.

Word list for word-building, reading and spelling:
end, imp, and, ink, its, opt, ant, alp, act, elm, asp, elk, amp

Book 1: Reading and spelling VCC words

imp	✓	___ ___ ___	
end		___ ___ ___	
ink		___ ___ ___	
opt		___ ___ ___	
and		___ ___ ___	
elf		___ ___ ___	
its		___ ___ ___	
alp		___ ___ ___	
elk		___ ___ ___	

Teaching aims: Reading and spelling VCC words

Teaching guidelines: Fold this sheet along the dotted line. Ask the student to read the words on the left and check off the words she/he has read correctly. Ask the student to turn over the sheet and dictate the words to the student. Ask the student to spell the words by segmenting and sounding out the sounds as she/he writes them on the lines. Ask the student to open the sheet and check off the words she/he has spelled correctly.

Book 1: VCC words

Reading accuracy

den
end
bed

its
sad
sit

kin
ink
imp

act
cat
cot

map
amp
Pam

opt
top
pot

Teaching aims: Reading accuracy

Teaching guidelines: Ask the student to read the words in each box and circle the word that matches the picture.

Book 1: VCC nonsense words

Full circle game: playing with sounds

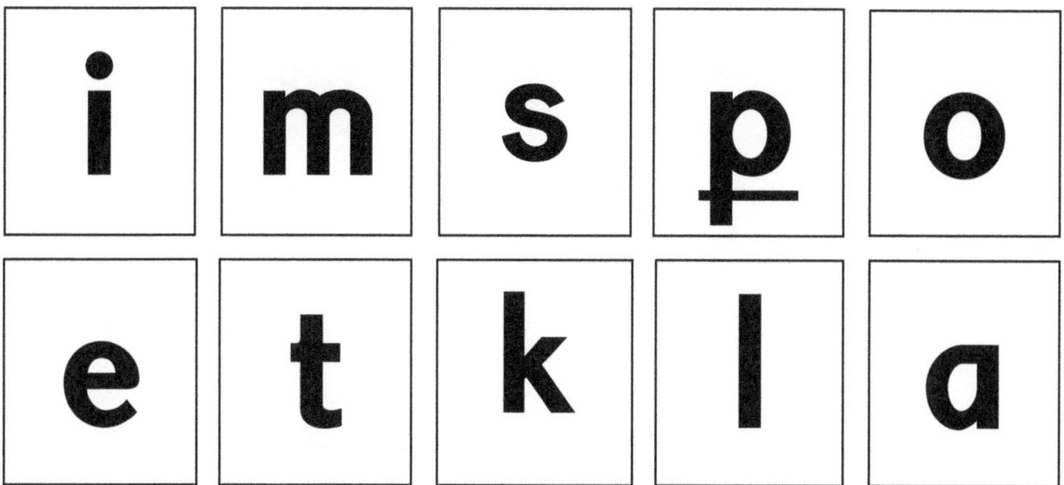

im > ims > ips > ip > ep > eps > ops > ots > os > osk > esk > isk > ilk > elk > alk > alp > elp > ilp > il > im

Teaching aims: Practice manipulating sounds in VCC nonsense words.

Teaching point: Manipulating sounds in nonsense words is a useful activity for older students as they are required to listen to sounds in words they have not seen before and therefore cannot rely on their visual memory. This develops their ability to segment sounds in words.

Teaching guidelines: Ask the student to build the word 'im', using the cards above. Explain they will be building nonsense words. You are going to ask them to change one sound in the word to make a new word. He/she may need to add, take out or change a sound in the word. Ask the student to listen carefully to the new word and change it according to how it sounds. The word may be a real word or a nonsense word. Once the student has built the word, ask him/her to read it. Complete the activity until the student has returned to the original word 'im'.

Book 1: VCC words

Reading captions

1. an act on a box

2. a tub and a pup

3. ink in a pot

4. an ant on a bud

5. a man on an alp

6. a hat on an elf

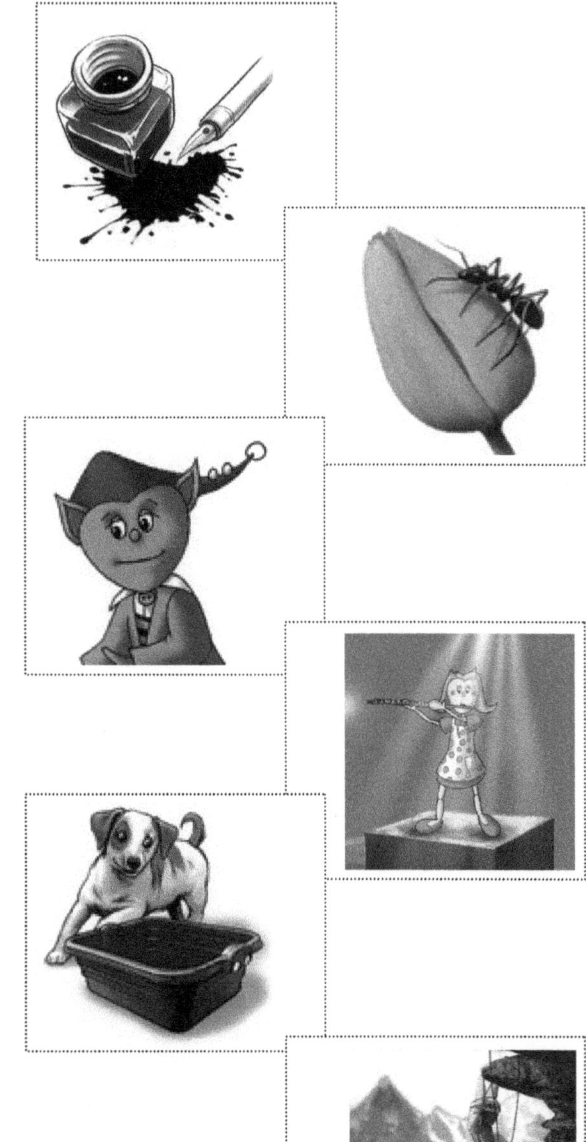

Teaching aims: Reading captions and comprehension

Teaching guidelines: Ask the student to read the captions and draw a line to the matching picture.

Teaching point: When reading high-frequency words, point to the grapheme the student does not yet know and sound it out for the student, e.g. with the word 'the', sound out 'th' and the shwa sound 'th'.

Book 1: VCC words

Writing captions

1. __ __   __ __ __   __ __   __   __ __ __

2. __   __ __ __   __ __ __   __   __ __ __

3. __ __ __   __ __   __   __ __ __

4. __ __   __ __ __   __ __   __   __ __ __

5. __   __ __ __   __ __   __ __   __ __ __

6. __   __ __ __   __ __   __ __   __ __ __

Teaching aims: Writing and spelling captions with VCC words

Guidelines: Dictate the captions from the previous page to the student. Ask him/her to listen to the sounds in the words and say them as he/she writes them on the lines.

Book 1: Reading and spelling two-syllable words

Word	✓	Spelling	
lap/top	✓	____/____	
bed/bug		____/____	
Bat/man		____/____	
cat/nap		____/____	
ad/mit		___/____	
ban/dit		____/____	
ex/it		___/___	
kid/nap		____/____	
cab/in		____/___	

Teaching aims: Reading and spelling words with CVC syllables

Teaching guidelines: Fold this sheet along the dotted line. Ask the student to read the words on the left and check off the words she/he has read correctly. Ask the student to turn over the sheet and dictate the words to the student. Ask the student to spell the words by segmenting and sounding out the sounds as she/he writes them on the lines. Ask the student to open the sheet and check off the words she/he has spelled correctly.

Book 1: Comprehension: Spot it!

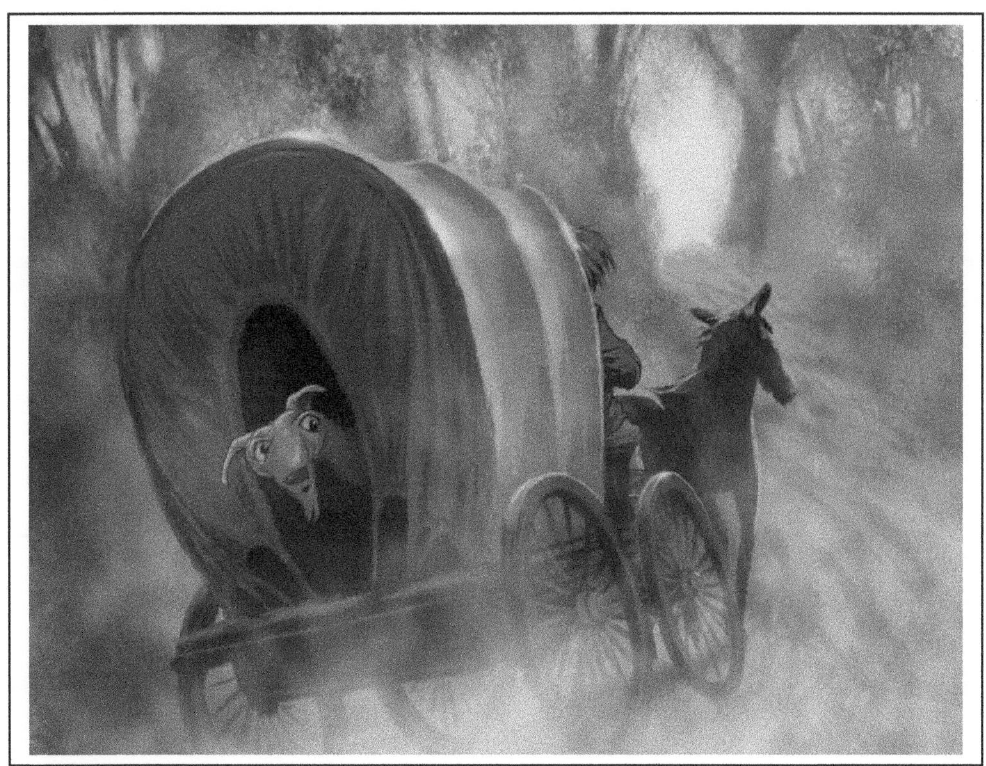

1. Can you spot the wagon?	yes	no
2. Is the kid in the wagon?	yes	no
3. Can you spot Grandpa?	yes	no
4. Is Zak on the wagon?	yes	no
5. Can you spot the man in the red hat?	yes	no
6. Can you spot the nag?	yes	no
7. Is the sun up?	yes	no

Teaching guidelines:
This is a comprehension activity. Ask the student to look at the picture and answer the questions. He/she must then circle the words yes or no.
Words the student may need help with: you, the, is

Book 1: Comprehension 2: Sequence the story

1.

2.

3.

4.

5.

6.

Zak sets off in the wagon to get help.

Zak gets up. Grandpa cannot get up. He is not well.

Zak can see a man in the fog. He has a big, red hat.

The wagon jogs on. The man hums and pats his rat.

Zak fixes the wagon to the nag.

Zak lets the man onto the wagon. The man is odd.

Teaching guidelines:
Cut up the sentences above. Ask the student to read the sentences carefully and sequence them in the order of the story in Book 1, 'The Man in the Mist'. The student then sticks them in the numbered boxes in the correct order.
Words the student may need help with: the, to, he, is, his, see, a, has

Book 1: Comprehension 3: Fill in the missing words

rat	pats	hat	fog
belt	lamp	box	help

Zak sets off to get _ _ _ _. The wagon jogs on.

A man in the _ _ _! The man has a red _ _ _

on. The man lifts a _ _ _ _. The man gets on

the wagon. The man has a _ _ _ _ on his hips.

He has a _ _ _ on his lap. In the box is a

_ _ _. The man hums and _ _ _ _ the rat.

Teaching guidelines:
Ask the student to read the text and fill in the missing words. He/she should sound out the words as they write them on the lines. He/she can cross out the words in the boxes above as they use them in the text.

Book 1: Writing frame

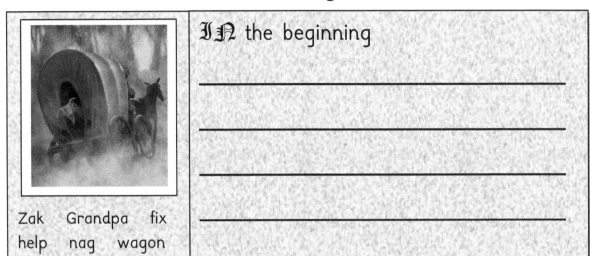

Zak Grandpa fix
help nag wagon

IN the beginning

____

____

____

____

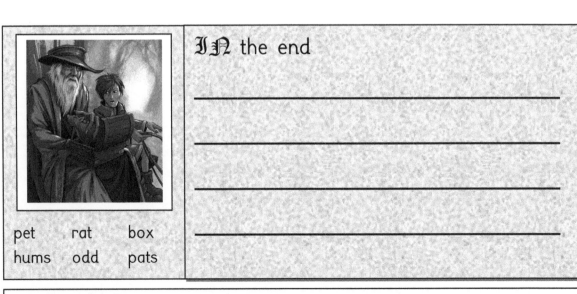

mist man belt
red hat wagon

IN the middle

____

____

____

____

pet rat box
hums odd pats

IN the end

____

____

____

____

Teaching guidelines: Above is a writing frame to help the student to sequence the story. Some words are provided under the images to support spelling.

Book 1: Vocabulary

New words in Book 1:

dim – faintly lit, difficult to see
nag – old horse
kid – a young goat
kin – a person's family
odd – strange

Zak had a	the dim fog.
Zak had no mom and	was cold and wet.
Zak set off in	dad. Grandpa was his kin.
The man in the red hat	pet kid.
It was not hot. It	to the wagon.
Zak had to fix the nag	ten slots in it.
The belt had	was odd.

Teaching guidelines:
This activity includes new vocabulary introduced in Book 1, 'The Man in the Mist'. It encourages the student to think about the meaning of the new words and to use them to construct a complete sentence. Cut the sentences into strips and cut along the dotted line. Ask the student to match the two parts of the sentence so that they make sense. The student may need a reminder of what the words mean.

Book 1: Punctuation activity

The sun is up zak sits up in bed grandpa cannot get up he is not well

zak sets off to get help it is cold and wet zak can see a man in the mist

the man has a red hat on the man has a box in the box is a pet rat

Did you spot?

10 missing full stops

9 missing capital letters

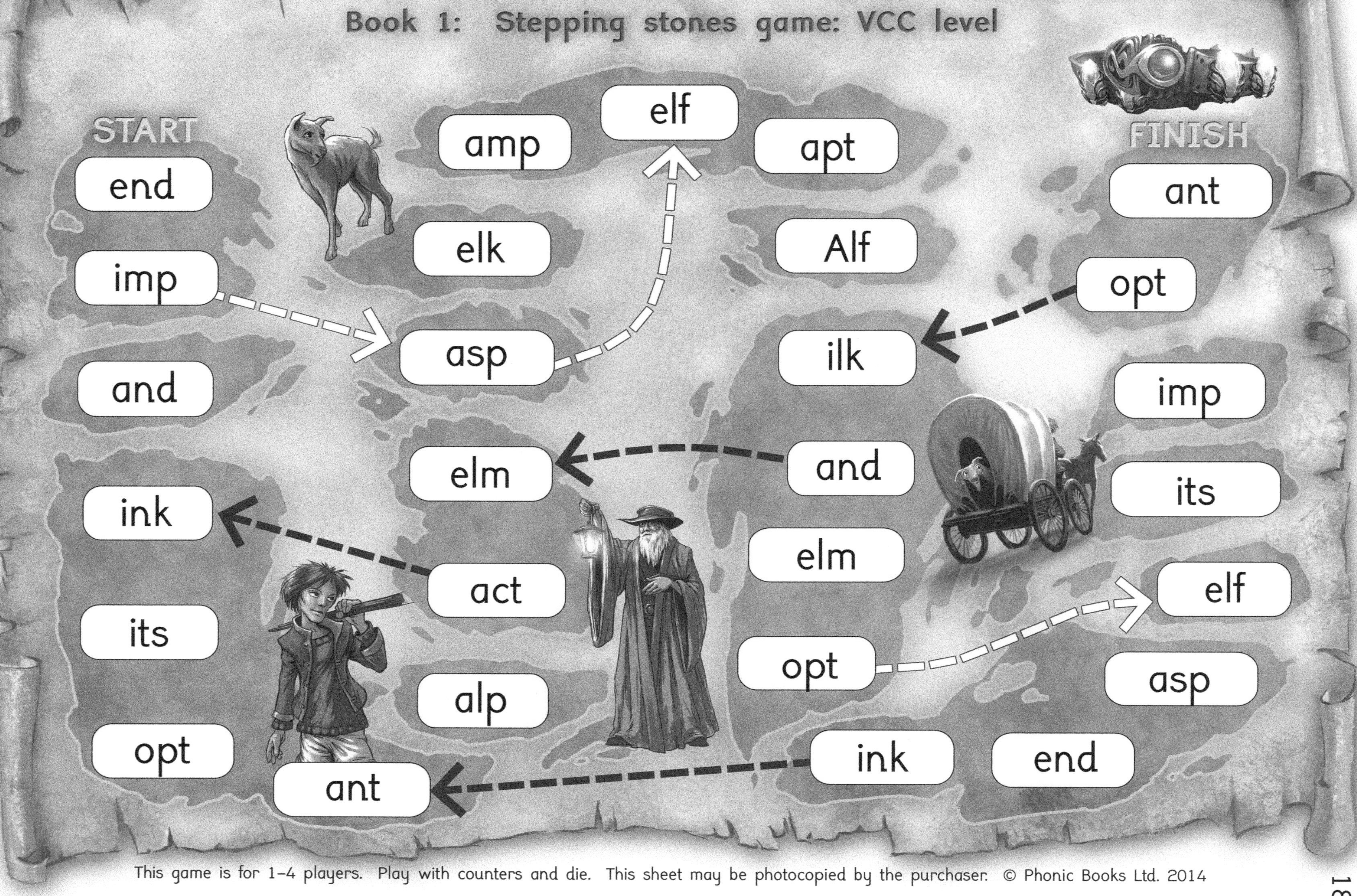

This game is for 1–4 players. Play with counters and die. This sheet may be photocopied by the purchaser.

Book 2: Ten Rocks

Questions for discussion

Chapter 1

1. What does the man in the red hat tell Zak? (pp. 1, 2)
2. How do you think he knows that Grandpa is not well? (p. 1)
3. What does he leave behind when he disappears? (p. 3)

Chapter 2

1. What is the map for? (p. 4)
2. What does Zak ask his pal, Finn? (p. 6)
3. Why do you think Zak might be disappointed? (p. 6)

Chapter 3

1. What does Zak pack? (p. 7)
2. Why is Grandpa upset? (p. 8)

Chapter 4

1. Who jumps on top of Zak? (p. 10)
2. What do you think Zak feels when Finn tells him he can come on the quest? (p. 11)

Teaching guidelines:
These questions can be discussed after reading the text. They will help develop speaking and listening skills, comprehension and vocabulary.

Book 2: Word-building CVCC words

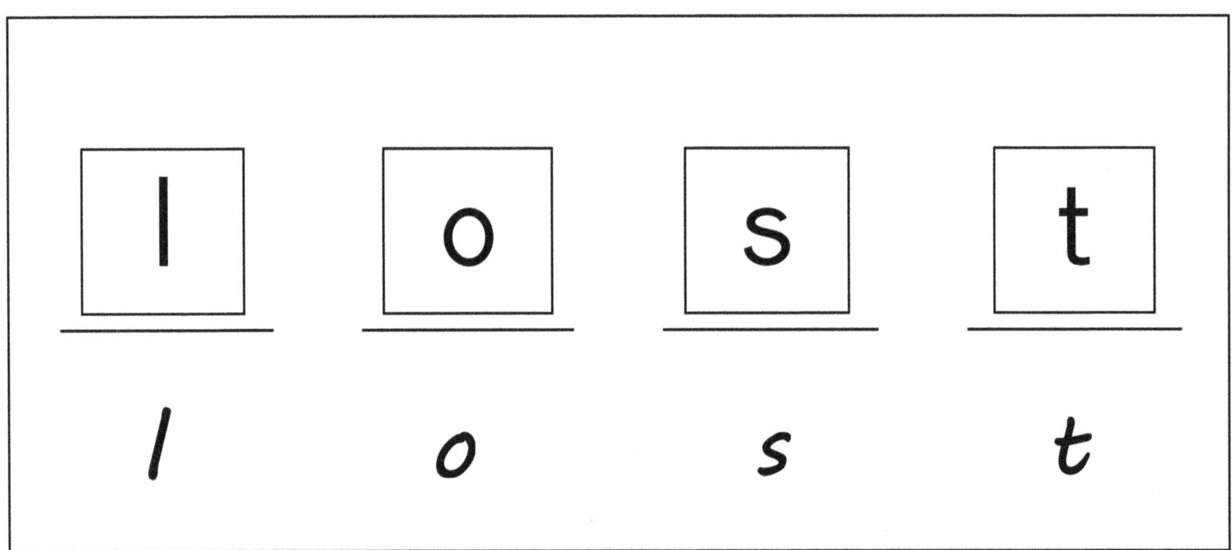

Teaching aims:

- Segment and blend CVCC (consonant/vowel/consonant/consonant) words with the sounds of the alphabet.

Teacher guidelines:
Use a white board on which four lines have been drawn. Use the cards from the introductory levels for word-building.

Teach word-building
Select a word from the list below. Use only the letters needed to build that word and jumble them up. Ask the student to build that word by listening to the sounds in the word and segmenting all the sounds in the word, one at a time. The student then places each card on the appropriate line once he/she has segmented the word. Ask the student to read the word he/she has built. Ask the student to write the word under the lines, saying the sounds as he/she does.

Word list for word-building, reading and spelling:
lost, held, silk, melt, bump, nest, hand, bend, lift, rant, desk, wilt, ramp, west, sent, loft, honk, help, milk, damp, junk, rift, bond, tank, pond, wind, vest, yelp, zest, kept, tilt, cost, dust, lamp

Book 2: Reading and spelling CVCC words

lost	✓	___ ___ ___ ___	
held		___ ___ ___ ___	
damp		___ ___ ___ ___	
milk		___ ___ ___ ___	
junk		___ ___ ___ ___	
hand		___ ___ ___ ___	
went		___ ___ ___ ___	
tilt		___ ___ ___ ___	
cost		___ ___ ___ ___	

Teaching aims: Reading and spelling CVCC words

Teaching guidelines: Fold this sheet along the dotted line. Ask the student to read the words on the left and check off the words she/he has read correctly. Ask the student to turn over the sheet and dictate the words to the student. Ask the student to spell the words by segmenting and sounding out the sounds as she/he writes them on the lines. Ask the student to open the sheet and check off the words she/he has spelled correctly.

Book 2: CVCC words

Reading accuracy

 lots lost cost	 list lift tilt	 dust tubs bust
 sent tens tent	 damp maps bump	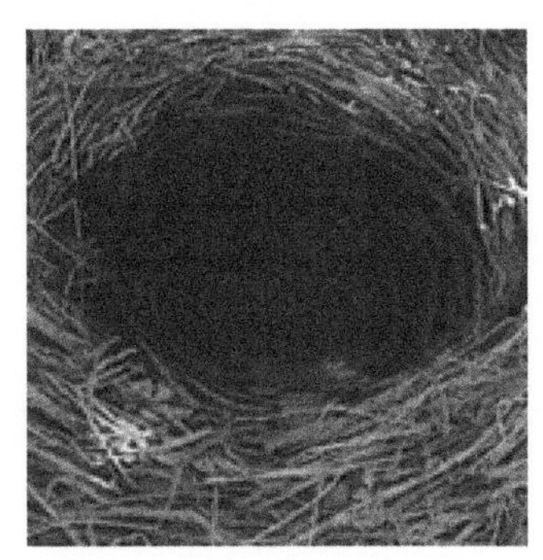 nets tens nest

Teaching aims: Reading accuracy

Teaching guidelines: Ask the student to read the words in each box and circle the word that matches the picture.

Book 2: CVCC nonsense words

Full circle game: playing with sounds

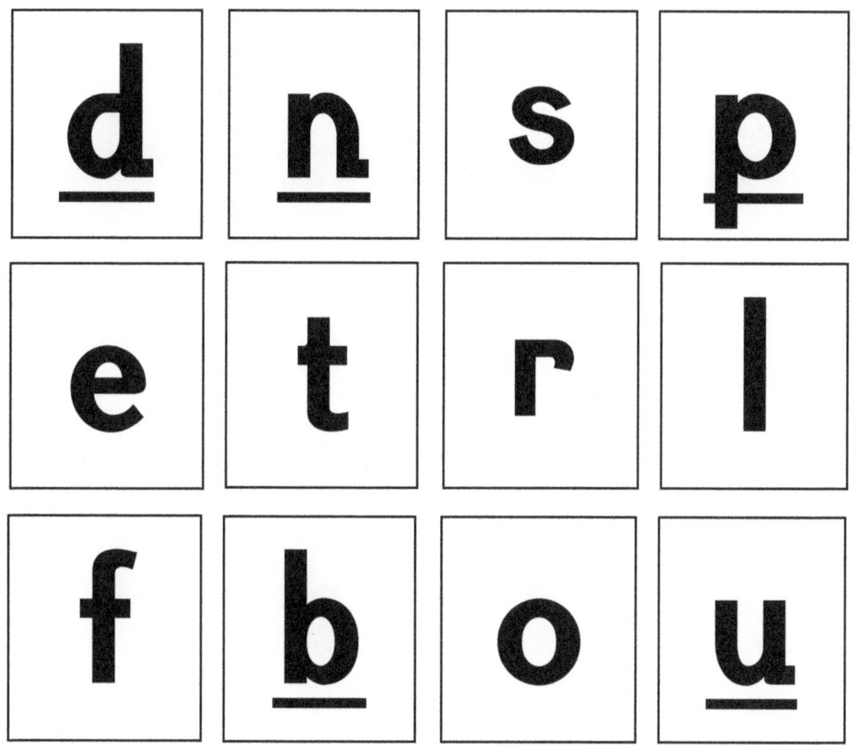

pont > punt > runt > rult > relt > rolt > rost > rot > rof > roft > reft > beft > boft > oft > ont > ond > end> lend > lent > lont > pont

Teaching aims: Practice manipulating sounds in CVCC nonsense words.

Teaching point: Manipulating sounds in nonsense words is a useful activity for older students as they are required to listen to sounds in words they have not seen before and therefore cannot rely on their visual memory. This develops their ability to segment sounds in words.

Teaching guidelines: Ask the student to build the word 'pont', using the cards above. Explain he/she will be building nonsense words. You are going to ask them to change one sound in the word to make a new word. He/she may need to add, take out or change a sound in the word. Ask the student to listen carefully to the new word and change it according to how it sounds. The word may be a real word or a nonsense word. Once the student has built the word, ask him/her to read it. Complete the activity until the student has returned to the original word 'pont'.

Book 2: CVCC words

Reading captions

1. a nest of eggs

2. dots on a pad

3. a wet, damp pet

4. a gust of wind

5. milk on a mat

6. a tent in a camp

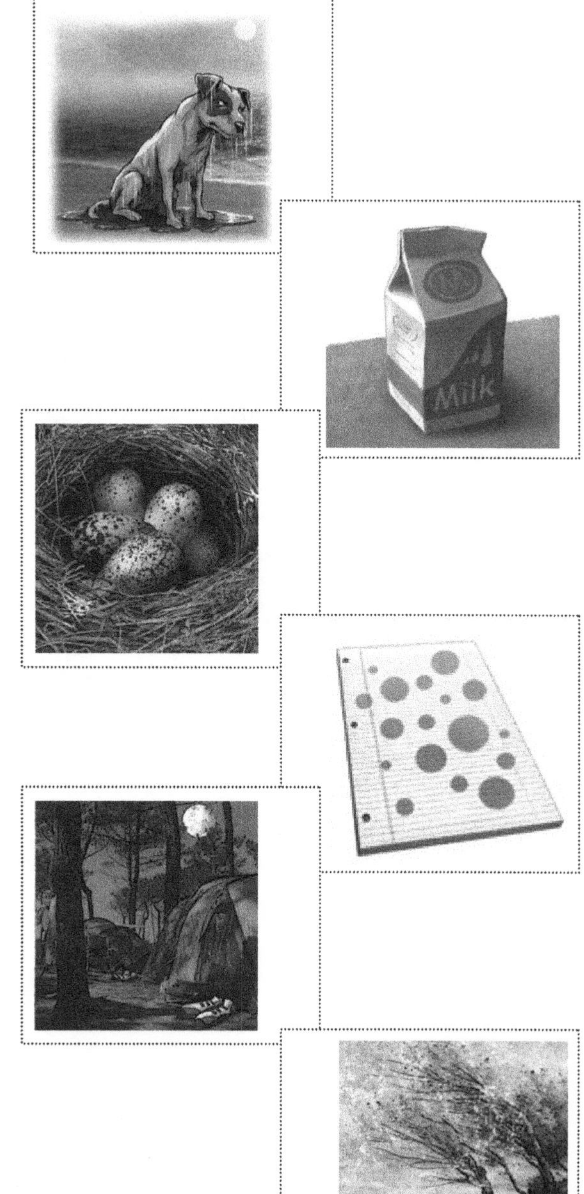

Teaching aims: Reading captions and comprehension

Teaching guidelines: Ask the student to read the captions and draw a line to the matching picture.

Teaching point: When reading high-frequency words, point to the grapheme the student does not yet know and sound it out for the student, e.g. with the word 'the', sound out 'th' and the shwa sound 'uh'.

Book 2: CVCC words

Writing captions

1. __   __ __ __ __   of   __ ___ __

2. __ __ __ __   __ __   __   __ __ __

3. __   __ __ __,   __ __ __ __   __ __ __

4. __   __ __ __ __   of   __ __ __ __

5. __ __ __ __   __ __   __   __ __ __

6. __   __ __ __ __   __ __   __   __ __ __ __

Teaching aims: Writing and spelling captions with CVCC words

Guidelines: Dictate the captions from the previous page to the student. Ask him/her to listen to the sounds in the words and say them as he/she writes them on the lines.

Book 2: Reading and spelling two-syllable words

in/sult	✓	___/____	
end/less		____/______	
den/tist		____/______	
wind/mill		______/______	
con/tact		____/______	
sand/pit		______/____	
in/sect		___/______	
sus/pect		____/______	
ob/ject		___/______	

Teaching aims: Reading and spelling words with CVCC syllables

Teaching guidelines: Fold this sheet along the dotted line. Ask the student to read the words on the left and check off the words she/he has read correctly. Ask the student to turn over the sheet and dictate the words to the student. Ask the student to spell the words by segmenting and sounding out the sounds as she/he writes them on the lines. Ask the student to open the sheet and check off the words she/he has spelled correctly.

Book 2: Comprehension: Spot it!

1. Can you spot the cup?	yes	no
2. Can you spot the map?	yes	no
3. Is the cup on the map?	yes	no
4. Can you spot a rug?	yes	no
5. Is the belt next to the rug?	yes	no
6. Can you spot a lamp?	yes	no
7. Is the bag in the wagon?	yes	no

Teaching guidelines:
This is a comprehension activity. Ask the student to look at the picture and answer the questions. He/she must then circle the words yes or no.

Book 2: Comprehension 2: Sequence the story

1.

2.

3.

4.

5.

6.

Finn jumps on top of Zak.

Zak asks Finn to come, but Finn cannot.

Zak gets a rug, cup, map and the belt.

Zak and Finn set off.

The man in the red hat tells Zak about the magic belt.

The man has left a map and the belt on the wagon.

Teaching guidelines:
Cut up the sentences above. Ask the student to read the sentences carefully and sequence them in the order of the story in Book 2, 'Ten Rocks'. The student then sticks them in the numbered boxes in the correct order.
Words the student may need help with: of, to, come, a, the, about, magic

Book 2: Comprehension 3: Fill in the missing words

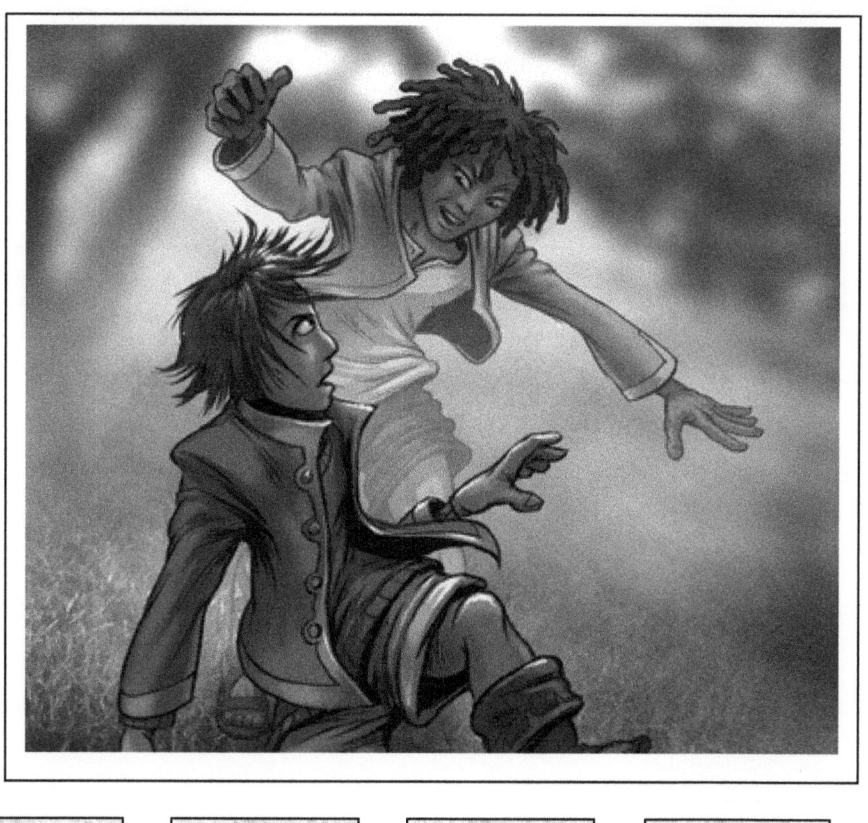

rob	sets	must	jumps
mud	upset	well	hug

Zak gives Grandpa a _ _ _. Grandpa is _ _ _ _ _. Can Zak help him get _ _ __? Zak _ _ _ _ off in the wagon. A lad _ _ _ _ _ on Zak. Zak lands in the _ _ _. Will the lad _ _ _ him? It is Finn. "Finn, get off! I _ _ _ _ get on!" Zak says.

Teaching guidelines:
Ask the student to read the text and fill in the missing words. He/she should sound out the words as they write them on the lines. He/she can cross out the words in the boxes above as they use them in the text.

Book 2: Writing frame

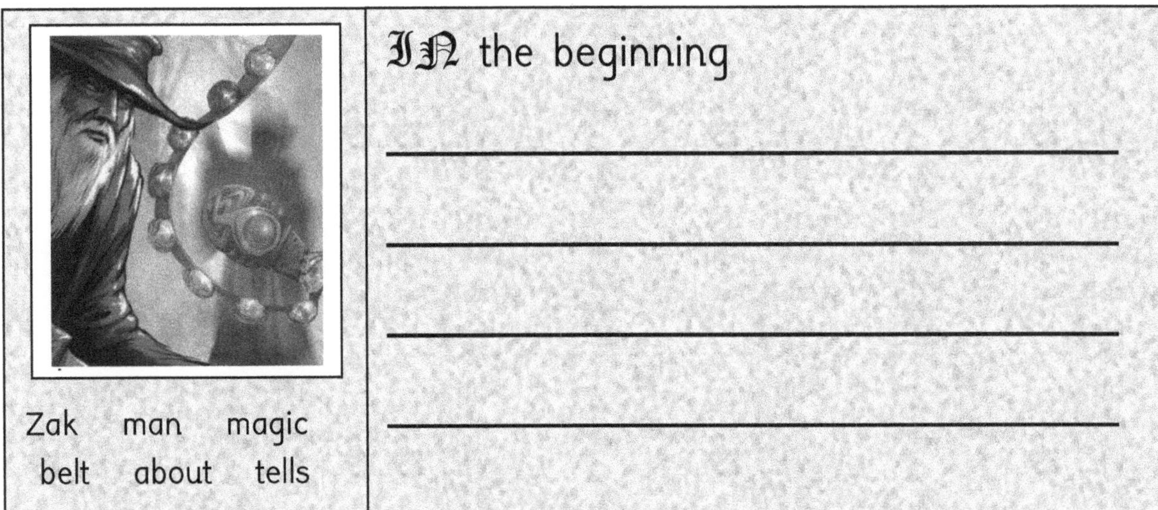

In the beginning
Zak man magic
belt about tells

In the middle

map mug bag
cup gets belt

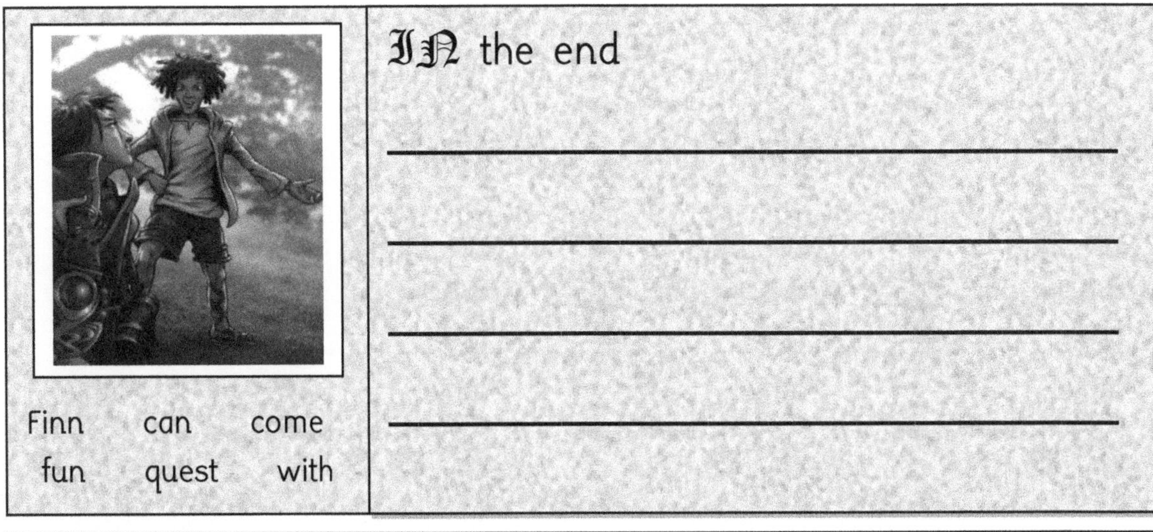

In the end
Finn can come
fun quest with

Teaching guidelines: Above is a writing frame to help the student to sequence the story. Some words are provided under the images to support spelling.

Book 2: Vocabulary

New words in Book 2:

nods – moves his head up and down to show he agrees
pal – friend
quest – a long search for something precious or valuable
begs – asks for something desperately

Zak begs Finn,	to get the ten rocks.
The man has left	he cannot come.
Finn tells Zak	man has hidden the rocks.
Finn jumps on	his pal, to come.
The man tells Zak a bad	set off. Grandpa nods.
Zak tells Grandpa he must	a map and a belt.
Zak sets off on a quest	top of Zak.

Teaching guidelines:
This activity includes new vocabulary introduced in Book 2, 'Ten Rocks'. It encourages the student to think about the meaning of the new words and to use them to construct a complete sentence. Cut the sentences into strips and cut along the dotted line. Ask the student to match the two parts of the sentence so that they make sense. The student may need a reminder of what the words mean.

Book 2: Punctuation activity

Zak gives grandpa a hug zak must set off grandpa is upset

zak sets off a lad jumps on top of him zak lands in the mud

zak tells finn to get off him zak and finn set off it is fun

Did you spot?

9 missing full stops

11 missing capital letters

Book 2: Stepping stones game: CVCC level

This game is for 1–4 players. Play with counters and die. This sheet may be photocopied by the purchaser.

Book 3: "Help Us!"

Questions for discussion

Chapter 1

1. Why does the belt slip off Zak? (p. 1)
2. How does Finn make the belt fit? (p. 2)

Chapter 2

1. Why does the rat bite Zak? (p. 3)
2. What does Finn want to do to the rat? (p. 3)
3. How does Rat help Zak and Finn? (p. 6)

Chapter 3

1. Why is the man running from the village? (p. 8)
2. Describe what the hogman is like. (p. 9)
3. Where is the magic gem? (p. 9)

Chapter 4

1. How does Finn save Zak? (p. 11)
2. What does Zak do when he gets the gem? (p. 12)

Teaching guidelines:
These questions can be discussed after reading the text. They will help develop speaking and listening skills, comprehension and vocabulary.

Book 3: Word-building more CVCC words

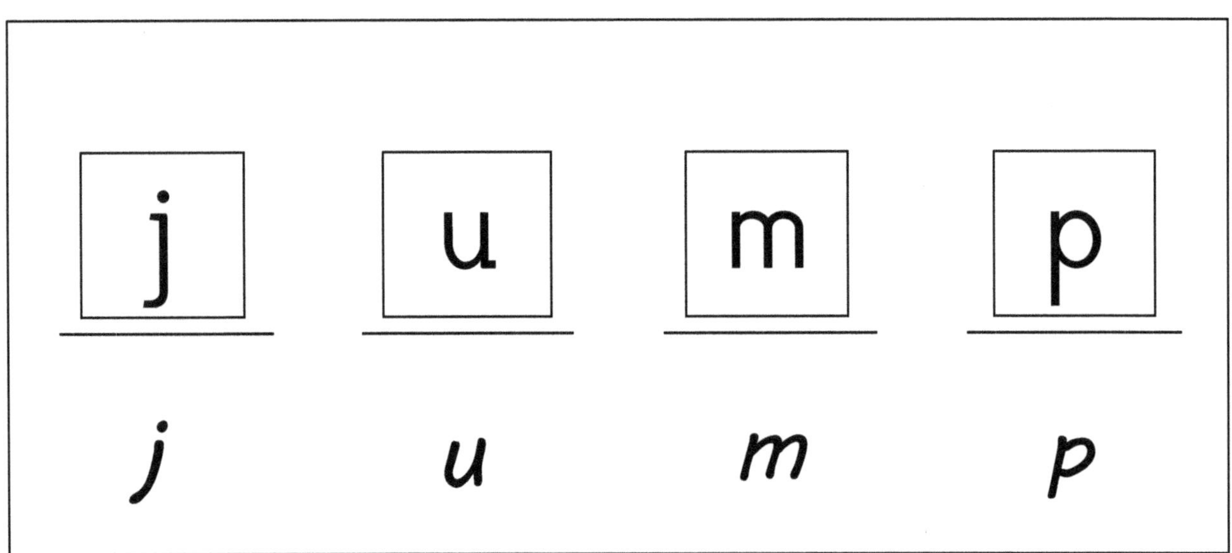

Teaching aims:

- Segment and blend CVCC (consonant/vowel/consonant/consonant) words with the sounds of the alphabet and double consonants.

Teacher guidelines:
Use a white board on which four lines have been drawn. Use the cards from the introductory levels.

Teach word-building
Select a word from the list below. Use only the letters needed to build that word and jumble them up. Ask the student to build that word by listening to the sounds in the word and segmenting all the sounds in the word, one at a time. The student then brings down each card once he/she has segmented the sound in the word. Ask the student to read the word he/she has built. Ask the student to write the word under the lines, saying the sounds as he/she does.

Word list for word-building, reading and spelling:
jump, limp, text, fond, just, pelt, land, mend, sand, rust, jolt, rent, gust, cats, lots, pins, must, film, gaps, puffs, huffs, cuffs, list, next, pant, lent, went, mint, hunt, mist, runt, pest, risk, tusk

Book 3: Reading and spelling CVCC words

Word	Read	Spelling	Spelled
jump	✓	___ ___ ___ ___	
held		___ ___ ___ ___	
link		___ ___ ___ ___	
band		___ ___ ___ ___	
pond		___ ___ ___ ___	
text		___ ___ ___ ___	
gaps		___ ___ ___ ___	
risk		___ ___ ___ ___	
dust		___ ___ ___ ___	

Teaching aims: Reading and spelling CVCC words

Teaching guidelines: Fold this sheet along the dotted line. Ask the student to read the words on the left and check off the words she/he has read correctly. Ask the student to turn over the sheet and dictate the words to the student. Ask the student to spell the words by segmenting and sounding out the sounds as she/he writes them on the lines. Ask the student to open the sheet and check off the words she/he has spelled correctly.

Book 3: More CVCC words

Reading accuracy

jump
pump
pups

pant
pans
snap

pest
test
pets

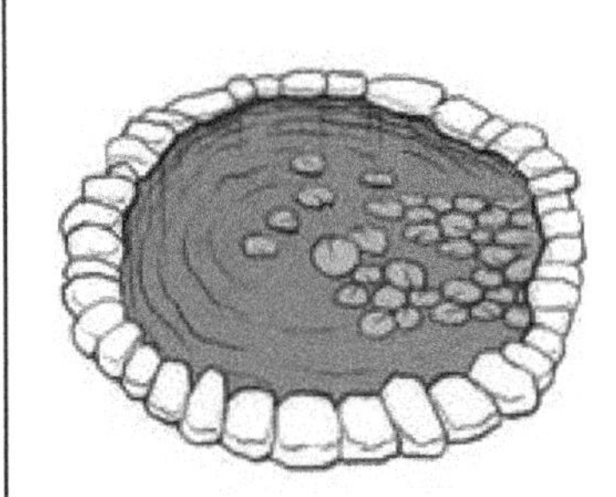

nods
pond
pops

list
slit
tills

pens
nips
pins

Teaching aims: Reading accuracy

Teaching guidelines: Ask the student to read the words in each box and circle the word that matches the picture.

Book 3: More CVCC nonsense words

Full circle game: playing with sounds

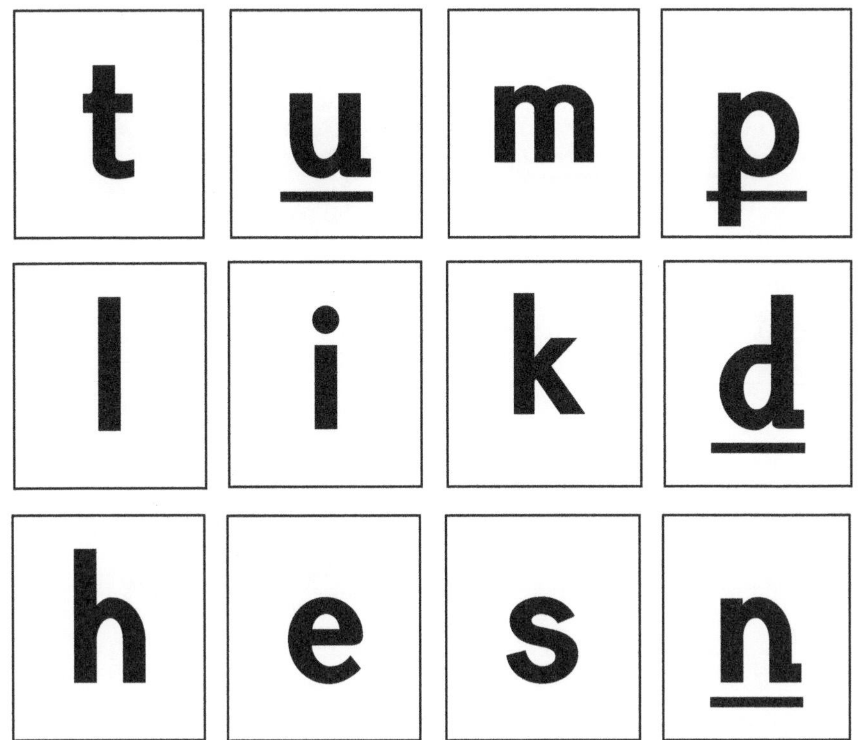

tump > tulp > tilp > milp > milk > ilk > ild > hild > held > eld > elt > est > dest > dent > den > des > dus > tus > tum > tump

Teaching aims: Practice manipulating sounds in CVCC nonsense words.

Teaching point: Manipulating sounds in nonsense words is a useful activity for older students as they are required to listen to sounds in words they have not seen before and therefore cannot rely on their visual memory. This develops their ability to segment sounds in words.

Teaching guidelines: Ask the student to build the word 'tump', using the cards above. Explain he/she will be building nonsense words. You are going to ask them to change one sound in the word to make a new word. He/she may need to add, take out or change a sound in the word. Ask the student to listen carefully to the new word and change it according to how it sounds. The word may be a real word or a nonsense word. Once the student has built the word, ask him/her to read it. Complete the activity until the student has returned to the original word 'tump'.

Book 3: More CVCC words

Reading captions

1. lots of tops

2. the best gift

3. a pen and a list

4. a kilt on a lad

5. a bunk bed

6. rats on a log

Teaching aims: Reading captions and comprehension

Teaching guidelines: Ask the student to read the captions and draw a line to the matching picture.

Teaching point: When reading high-frequency words, point to the grapheme the student does not yet know and sound it out for the student, e.g. with the word 'the', sound out 'th' and the shwa sound 'uh'.

Book 3: More CVCC words

Writing captions

1. _ _ _ _ of _ _ _ _

2. the _ _ _ _ _ _ _ _

3. _ _ _ _ _ _ _ _ _ _ _ _ _

4. _ _ _ _ _ _ _ _ _ _ _ _

5. _ _ _ _ _ _ _ _

6. _ _ _ _ _ _ _ _ _ _

Teaching aims: Writing and spelling captions with CVCC words

Guidelines: Dictate the captions from the previous page to the student. Ask him/her to listen to the sounds in the words and say them as he/she writes them on the lines.

Book 3: Reading and spelling two-syllable words

ab/sent	✓	___/______	
ant/hill		____/_____	
desk/top		_____/____	
pen/dant		____/_____	
con/text		____/_____	
con/vict		____/_____	
ex/ist		___/____	
in/vent		___/_____	
help/less		_____/_____	

Teaching aims: Reading and spelling words with VCC and CVCC syllables

Teaching guidelines: Fold this sheet along the dotted line. Ask the student to read the words on the left and check off the words she/he has read correctly. Ask the student to turn over the sheet and dictate the words to the student. Ask the student to spell the words by segmenting and sounding out the sounds as she/he writes them on the lines.Ask the student to open the sheet and check off the words she/he has spelled correctly.

Book 3: Comprehension: Spot it!

1. Can you spot the red rock?	yes	no
2. Can you spot the mud hut?	yes	no
3. Can you spot a big dog?	yes	no
4. Is Zak in the hut?	yes	no
5. Can you spot the hogman's tusks?	yes	no
6. Can you spot a tent?	yes	no
7. Is Finn on top of the mud hut?	yes	no

Teaching guidelines:
This is a comprehension activity. Ask the student to look at the picture and answer the questions. He/she must then circle the words yes or no.

Book 3: Comprehension 2: Sequence the story

1.

2.

3.

4.

5.

6.

Rat nips Zak on his hand.

Finn lifts Zak up and the hogman hits the mud hut.

The lads get to a village with mud huts.

The hogman runs at Zak.

A man runs from the village.

Zak tells Finn not to kill Rat as he will help them.

Teaching guidelines:
Cut up the sentences above. Ask the student to read the sentences carefully and sequence them in the order of the story in Book, "Help Us!". The student then sticks them in the numbered boxes in the correct order.
Words the student may need help with: his, the, to, a, village, with, as, he, them

Book 3: Comprehension 3: Fill in the missing words

hogman	tusks	hits	jumps
yanks	him	runs	hut

The hogman has the red rock in his _ _ _ _ _.

Zak yells at the _ _ _ _ _ _. Finn

_ _ _ _ _ on top of the hut. The hogman

_ _ _ _ at Zak. Finn _ _ _ _ _ Zak up. He

lifts _ _ _ up, just as the hogman _ _ _ _ the

mud _ _ _.

Teaching guidelines:
Ask the student to read the text and fill in the missing words. He/she should sound out the words as they write them on the lines. He/she can cross out the words in the boxes above as they use them in the text.

Book 3: Writing frame

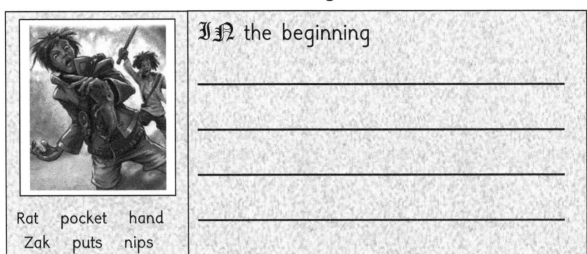

Rat pocket hand
Zak puts nips

In the beginning

____

____

____

____

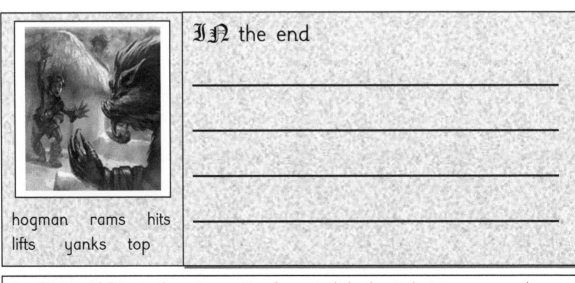

mud hut village
man runs help

In the middle

____

____

____

____

hogman rams hits
lifts yanks top

In the end

____

____

____

____

Teaching guidelines: Above is a writing frame to help the student to sequence the story. Some words are provided under the images to support spelling.

Book 3: Vocabulary

New words in Book 3:
village – a small group of houses in the country
hogman – a monster; half man, half pig
tusks – long, pointed teeth that stick out of an elephant, walrus or boar (wild pig)
rams – pushes one thing hard against another
yanks – pulls strongly and suddenly
dust it off – to brush the dust off something

The lads run	and fixes it to the belt.
The hogman has	top of the mud hut.
A man yells and runs	hits the mud hut.
Finn jumps on	to a village of mud huts.
Zak dusts off the red rock	and yanks him up.
The hogman	from the hogman.
Finn lifts Zak	the red rock in his tusks.

Teaching guidelines:
This activity includes new vocabulary introduced in Book 3, "Help Us!". It encourages the student to think about the meaning of the new words and to use them to construct a complete sentence. Cut the sentences into strips and cut along the dotted line. Ask the student to match the two parts of the sentence so that they make sense. The student may need a reminder of what the words mean.

Book 3: Punctuation activity

Finn gets on top of a hut zak yells at the hogman the hogman runs at him

finn gets on top of the hut he yanks zak up he lifts zak onto the top of the mud hut

the hogman hits the mud hut the red rock rolls into the dust

Did you spot?

8 missing full stops

9 missing capital letters

Book 3: Stepping stones game: CVCC level

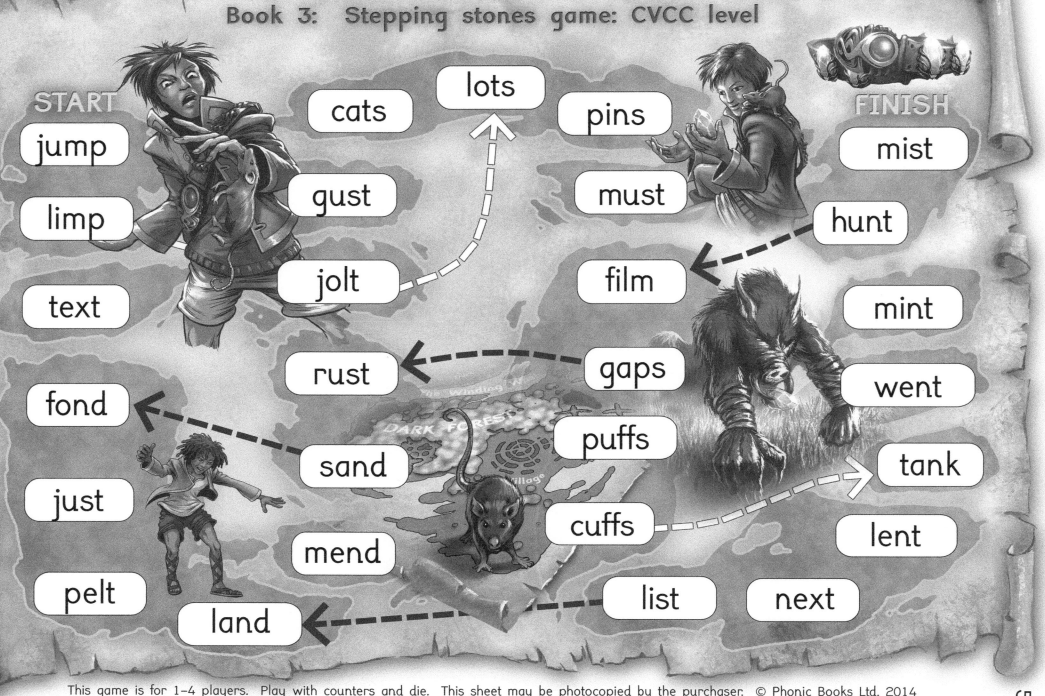

START

jump limp text fond just pelt

cats gust jolt rust sand mend land

lots pins must film gaps puffs cuffs list

next lent tank went mint hunt mist

FINISH

This game is for 1–4 players. Play with counters and die. This sheet may be photocopied by the purchaser.

Book 4: The Clam

Questions for discussion

Chapter 1

1. Why do you think Zak felt smug? (p. 1)
2. Why do you think this made Finn cross? (p. 2)

Chapter 2

1. Who was guarding the clam? (p. 5)
2. "The pink rock was snug in the clam." What does that mean? (p. 6)
3. Why does the river change color? (p. 6)

Chapter 3

1. What does the river cat do when Finn gets the clam? (p. 8)

Chapter 4

1. What does the word 'glint' mean? (p. 10)
2. Why do you think the river cat slinks off? (p. 11)
3. Why does Zak say: "No, *we* got it!" at the end? (p. 12)

Teaching guidelines:
These questions can be discussed after reading the text. They will help develop speaking and listening skills, comprehension and vocabulary.

Book 4: Word-building CCVC words

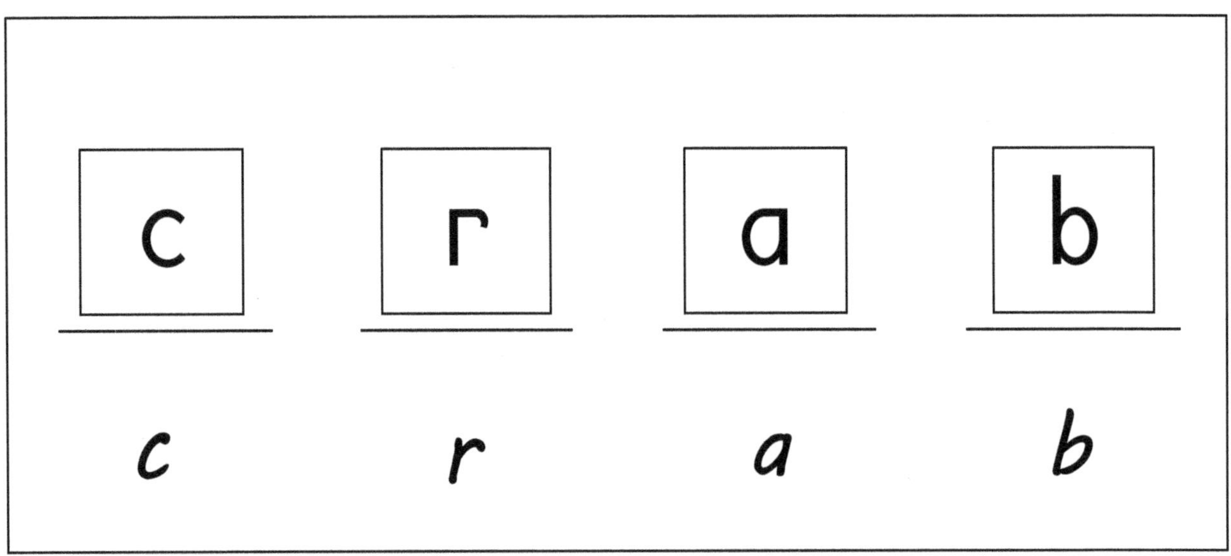

Teaching aims:

- Segment and blend CCVC (consonant/consonant/vowel/consonant) words with the sounds of the alphabet and double consonants.

Teacher guidelines:
Use a white board on which four lines have been drawn. Use the cards from the introductory levels.

Teach word-building
Select a word from the list below. Use only the letters needed to build that word and jumble them up. Ask the student to build that word by listening to the sounds in the word and segmenting all the sounds in the word, one at a time. The student then brings down each card once he/she has segmented the sound in the word. Ask the student to read the word he/she has built. Ask the student to write the word under the lines, saying the sounds as he/she does.

Word list for word-building, reading and spelling:
Crab, slip, stop, grub, sled, plum, snap, step, from, blip, drip, drag, stun, cram, gran, drug, slap, blob, flan, snip, bled, fret, slam, blot, drop, tram, slot, plot, trot, brag, clan, glen, flip

Book 4: Reading and spelling CCVC words

Word	✓	Spelling	✓
crab	✓	___ ___ ___ ___	
drip		___ ___ ___ ___	
step		___ ___ ___ ___	
plot		___ ___ ___ ___	
glug		___ ___ ___ ___	
bran		___ ___ ___ ___	
stem		___ ___ ___ ___	
trim		___ ___ ___ ___	
slot		___ ___ ___ ___	

Teaching aims: Reading and spelling CCVC words

Teaching guidelines: Fold this sheet along the dotted line. Ask the student to read the words on the left and check off the words she/he has read correctly. Ask the student to turn over the sheet and dictate the words to the student. Ask the student to spell the words by segmenting and sounding out the sounds as she/he writes them on the lines. Ask the student to open the sheet and check off the words she/he has spelled correctly.

Book 4: CCVC words

Reading accuracy

brag
grab
bran

snip
nips
pins

pots
stop
tops

plum
lump
pulp

stun
nuts
suns

slip
lisp
lips

Teaching aims: Reading accuracy

Teaching guidelines: Ask the student to read the words in each box and circle the word that matches the picture.

Book 4: CCVC nonsense words

Full circle game: playing with sounds

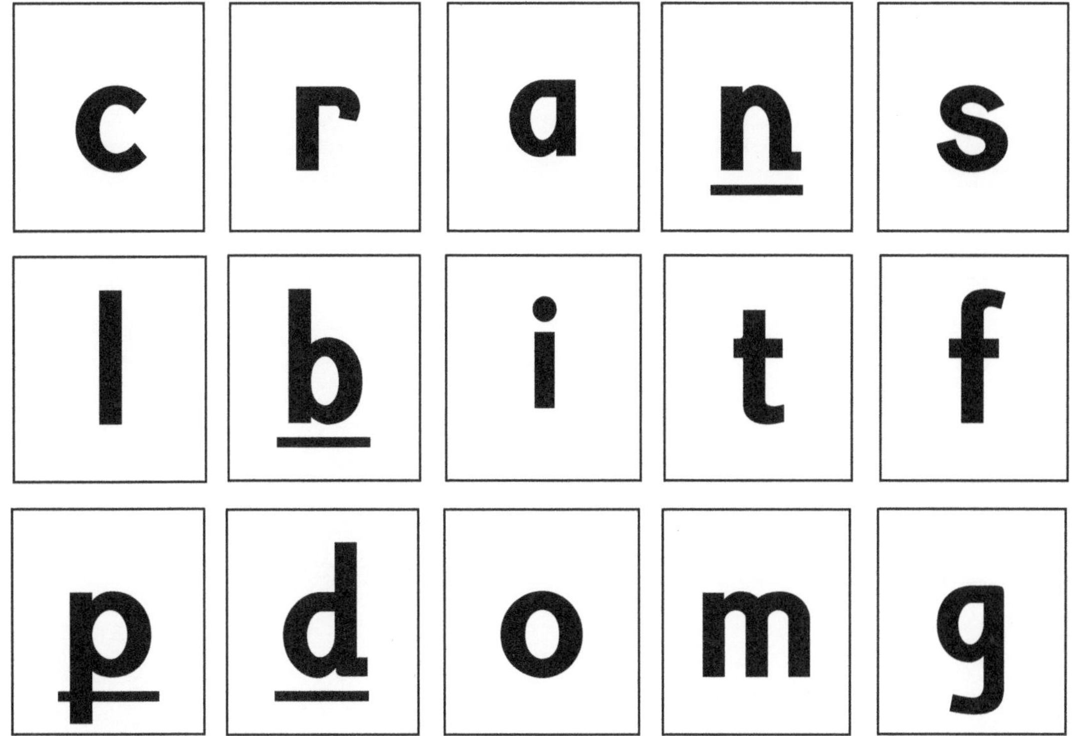

cran > clan < lan > blan > bran > brin > trin > prin > prit > plit > pit > rit > drit > drot > drom> dom > om > som > stom > slom > flom > flob > frob > frib > grib > grab > glab > clab > crab > cran

Teaching aims: Practice manipulating sounds in CCVC nonsense words.

Teaching point: Manipulating sounds in nonsense words is a useful activity for older students as they are required to listen to sounds in words they have not seen before and therefore cannot rely on their visual memory. This develops their ability to segment sounds in words.

Teaching guidelines: Ask the student to build the word 'cran', using the cards above. Explain he/she will be building nonsense words. You are going to ask them to change one sound in the word to make a new word. He/she may need to add, take out or change a sound in the word. Ask the student to listen carefully to the new word and change it according to how it sounds. The word may be a real word or a nonsense word. Once the student has built the word, ask him/her to read it. Complete the activity until the student has returned to the original word 'cran'.

Book 4: CCVC words

Reading captions

1. a frog in a pond

2. a damp slug

3. a scab on a leg

4. crab in the sand

5. a flag flaps

6. sled on a ramp

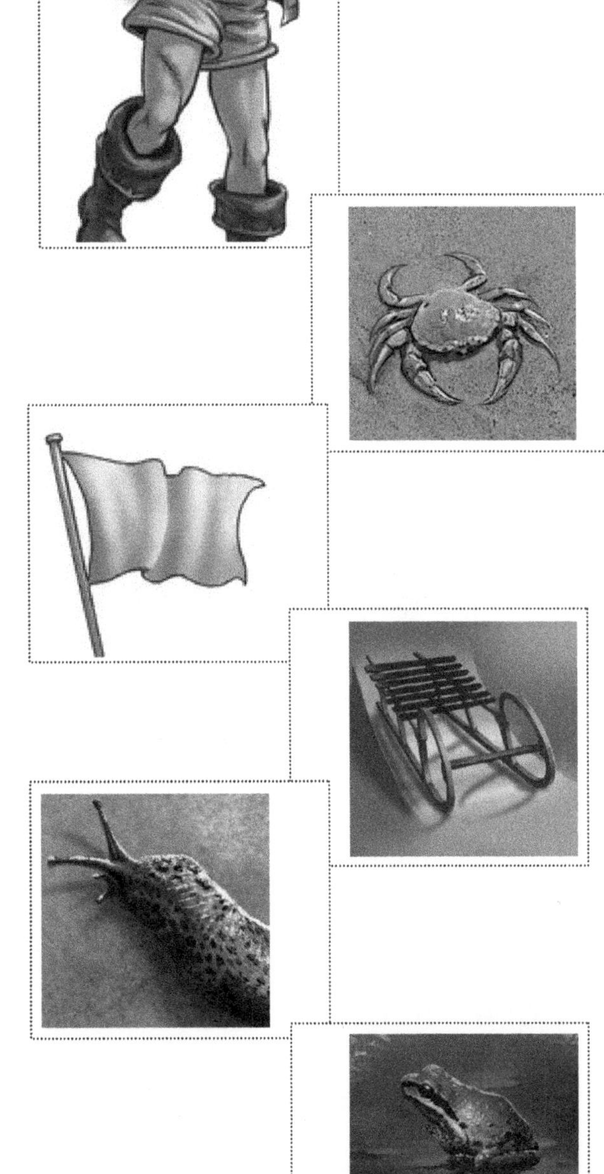

Teaching aims: Reading captions and comprehension

Teaching guidelines: Ask the student to read the captions and draw a line to the matching picture.

Teaching point: When reading high-frequency words, point to the grapheme the student does 'not yet know and sound it out for the student, e.g. with the word 'the', sound out 'th' and the shwa sound 'uh'.

Book 4: CCVC words

Writing captions

1. _ _ _ _ _ _ _ _ _ _ _ _

2. _ _ _ _ _ _ _ _ _

3. _ _ _ _ _ _ _ _ _ _ _

4. _ _ _ _ _ _ the _ _ _ _

5. _ _ _ _ _ _ _ _ _ _

6. _ _ _ _ _ _ _ _ _ _ _

Teaching aims: Writing and spelling captions with CVCC words

Guidelines: Dictate the captions from the previous page to the student. Ask him/her to listen to the sounds in the words and say them as he/she writes them on the lines.

Book 4: Reading and spelling two-syllable words

Word	✓	Spelling	✓
frog/man	✓	_ _ _ _/_ _ _	
com/plex		_ _ _/_ _ _ _	
cred/it		_ _ _ _/_ _	
frag/ment		_ _ _ _/_ _ _ _	
drop/lets		_ _ _ _/_ _ _ _	
un/dress		_ _/_ _ _ _ _	
trip/let		_ _ _ _/_ _ _	
stun/gun		_ _ _ _/_ _ _	
in/step		_ _/_ _ _ _	

Teaching aims: Reading and spelling words with CCVC syllables.

Teaching guidelines: Fold this sheet along the dotted line. Ask the student to read the words on the left and check off the words she/he has read correctly. Ask the student to turn over the sheet and dictate the words to the student. Ask the student to spell the words by segmenting and sounding out the sounds as she/he writes them on the lines. Ask the student to open the sheet and check off the words she/he has spelled correctly.

Book 4: The three sounds of '–ed'

t	d	id

skipped	jumped	tripped
landed	hugged	spotted
rubbed	panted	scanned
puffed	yelled	lifted
snapped	skidded	grabbed

Teaching guidelines: This can be used as a sorting game or as a written activity. First, discuss verbs in the past, present and future tenses and explain that –ed is an ending for the past tense. Ask the student to listen carefully to the sound of –ed at the end of each word and write the word in the correct column. This will help the student with spelling.
To make a game, photocopy this sheet onto card to make one card for each player. Place the word cards upside down in a pile. Players take turns to pick one up. The first to have three cards in each box is the winner.

Book 4: Comprehension: Spot it!

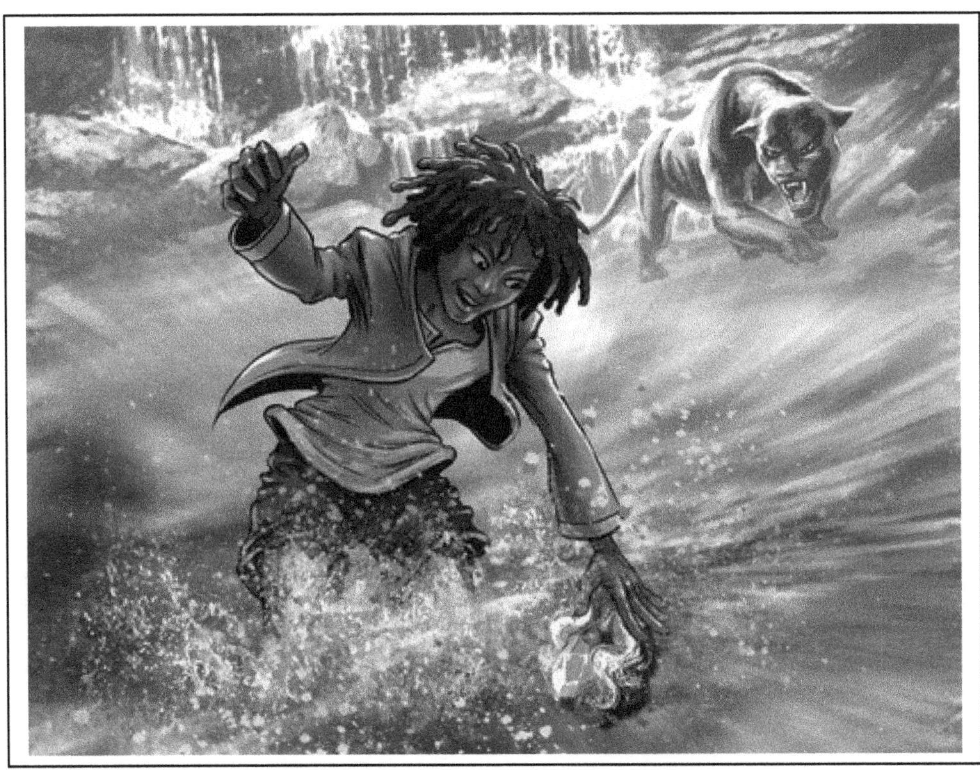

1. Can you spot Zak?	yes	no
2. Can you spot Finn?	yes	no
3. Has Finn got the belt?	yes	no
4. Can you spot the magic rock?	yes	no
5. Is the rock in the clam?	yes	no
6. Has the big cat jumped on Finn?	yes	no
7. Has the rock slipped from Finn's hand?	yes	no

Teaching guidelines:
This is a comprehension activity. Ask the student to look at the picture and answer the questions. He/she must then circle the words yes or no.

Book 4: Comprehension 2: Sequence the story

1.

2.

3.

4.

5.

6.

Zak grabbed the pink rock and the big cat slipped off.

Finn jumped in the river to get it.

Rat led the lads to a river and jumped in.

A pink rock was snug in the clam on the riverbed.

The rock slipped from his grip.

The river cat jumped onto Finn and dragged him off.

Teaching guidelines:
Cut up the sentences above. Ask the student to read the sentences carefully and sequence them in the order of the story in Book 4, 'The Clam'. The student then sticks them in the numbered boxes in the correct order.
Words the student may need help with: the, to, a, river, was, riverbed, his

Book 4: Comprehension 3: Fill in the missing words

dragged	jumped	grabbed	slipped
pink	fell	clam	from

Finn jumped in the river and _ _ _ __ __ the clam. He _ _ _ __ __. It _ _ __ from his hand. "I've got it!" Finn held up the _ _ _ _ in his hand. The river cat _ _ _ _ _ __ in the river. It grabbed Finn and _ _ _ __ __ him up the river. The _ _ _ _ rock fell _ _ _ _ the clam.

Teaching guidelines:
Ask the student to read the text and fill in the missing words. He/she should sound out the words as they write them on the lines. He/she can cross out the words in the boxes above as they use them in the text.

Book 4: Writing frame

pink rock snug
clam grab slipped

IN the beginning

____

____

____

____

river cat jumped
grabbed dragged

IN the middle

____

____

____

____

grabbed glint limp
let go slipped off

IN the end

____

____

____

____

Teaching guidelines: Above is a writing frame to help the student to sequence the story. Some words are provided under the images to support spelling.

Book 4: Vocabulary

New words in Book 4:
smug – to feel too pleased with oneself
admit – to agree that something is true
riverbank – the ground beside a river
clam – a large shellfish
riverbed – the bottom of the river
snug – fit comfortably
gasped – struggled to breathe

Zak had to admit	the river cat dragged him.
A clam rested on	in the clam.
Rat ran to a riverbank	with the rock in his belt.
The pink rock fell	and jumped in the river.
Zak felt a bit smug	the riverbed.
Finn gasped as	that Finn had helped him.
A pink rock was snug	from the clam.

Teaching guidelines:
This activity includes new vocabulary introduced in Book 4, 'The Clam'. It encourages the student to think about the meaning of the new words and to use them to construct a complete sentence. Cut the sentences into strips and cut along the dotted line. Ask the student to match the two parts of the sentence so that they make sense. The student may need a reminder of what the words mean.

Book 4: Punctuation activity

Zak jumped in and grabbed the rock it began to glint

the river cat went limp it let go of finn it slipped off

zak ran to help finn he grabbed his hand he yanked him from the river

Did you spot?

8 missing full stops

9 missing capital letters

Book 4: Stepping stones game: suffix –ed

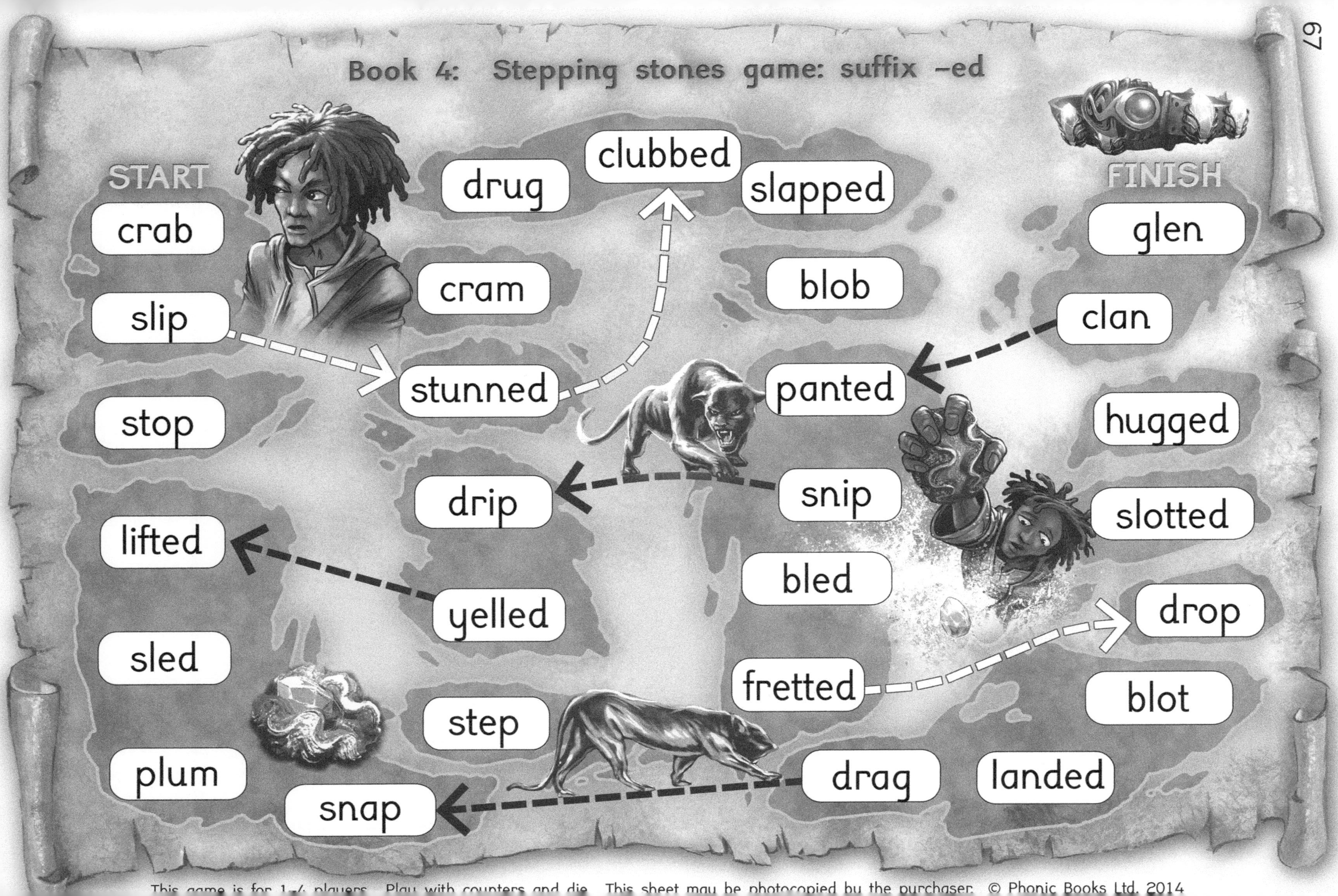

This game is for 1–4 players. Play with counters and die. This sheet may be photocopied by the purchaser.

Book 5: Crabs!

Questions for discussion

Chapter 1

1. What does the word 'slumped' mean? (p. 1)
2. Why did Zak prod Finn? (p. 3)

Chapter 2

1. The bog 'smelled rank'. What does that mean? (p. 4)
2. What was the bog like? (pp. 5, 6)
3. What happened to Finn in the bog? (p. 6)

Chapter 3

1. What does 'dank' mean? (p. 7)
2. What was the color of the magic rock Finn found? (p. 8)

Chapter 4

1. How did Zak get away from the crabs? (p. 10)
2. Why did Finn slip off the crabs? (p. 11)
3. How do you think that Rat found the magic rock? (p. 12)

Teaching guidelines:
These questions can be discussed after reading the text. They will help develop speaking and listening skills, comprehension and vocabulary.

Book 5: Word-building CCVCC words

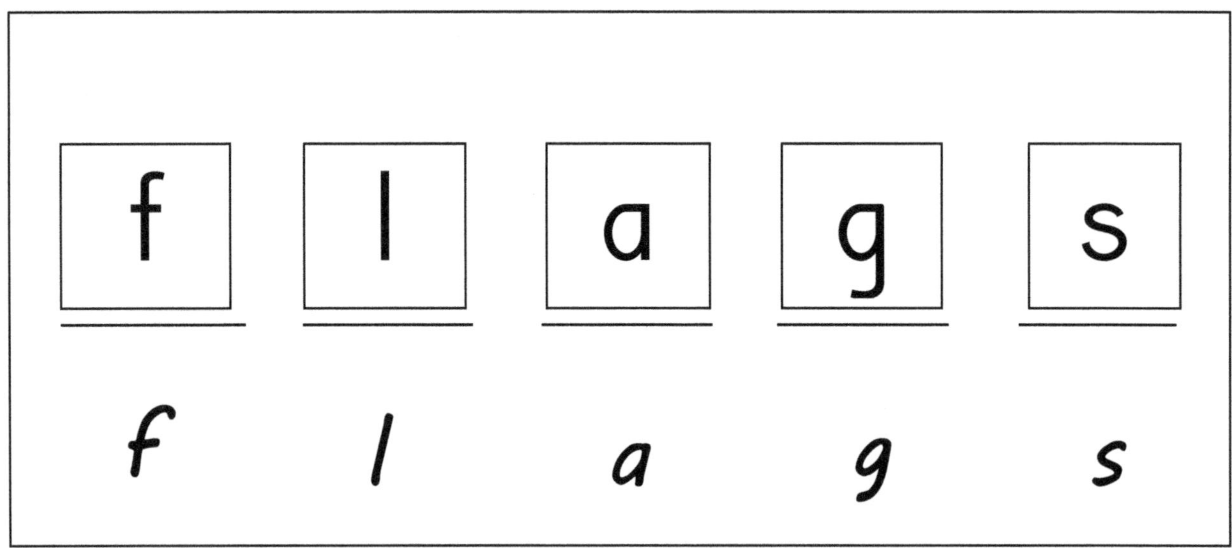

Teaching aims:

- Segment and blend CCVCC (consonant/consonant/vowel/consonant/consonant) words with the sounds of the alphabet.

Teacher guidelines:
Use a white board on which four lines have been drawn. Use the cards from the introductory levels.

Teach word-building
Select a word from the list below. Use only the letters needed to build that word and jumble them up. Ask the student to build that word by listening to the sounds in the word and segmenting all the sounds in the word, one at a time. The student then places each card on the appropriate line once he/she has segmented the word. Ask the student to read the word he/she has built. Ask the student to write the word under the lines, saying the sounds as he/she does.

Word list for word-building, reading and spelling:
flags, drank, swift, blond, tramp, plank, slump, slots, drips, stand, skunk, plump, grand, trump, crisp, trend, frost, grunt, twins, trust, bland, brand, clamp, print, prank, steps, stump, crest

Book 5: CCVCC words

Reading accuracy

slump
plums
lumps

twigs
twist
twins

pets
spells
steps

bland
band
sand

flags
glass
lags

pomp
stamp
stomp

Teaching aims: Reading accuracy

Teaching guidelines: Ask the student to read the words in each box and circle the word that matches the picture.

Book 5: Reading and spelling CCVCC words

Word	✓	Spelling	✓
flags	✓	_ _ _ _ _	
drink		_ _ _ _ _	
slump		_ _ _ _ _	
spots		_ _ _ _ _	
print		_ _ _ _ _	
frost		_ _ _ _ _	
trend		_ _ _ _ _	
crisp		_ _ _ _ _	
clamp		_ _ _ _ _	

Teaching aims: Reading and spelling CCVCC words

Teaching guidelines: Fold this sheet along the dotted line. Ask the student to read the words on the left and check off the words she/he has read correctly. Ask the student to turn over the sheet and dictate the words to the student. Ask the student to spell the words by segmenting and sounding out the sounds as she/he writes them on the lines. Ask the student to open the sheet and check off the words she/he has spelled correctly.

Book 5: CCVCC nonsense words

Full circle game: playing with sounds

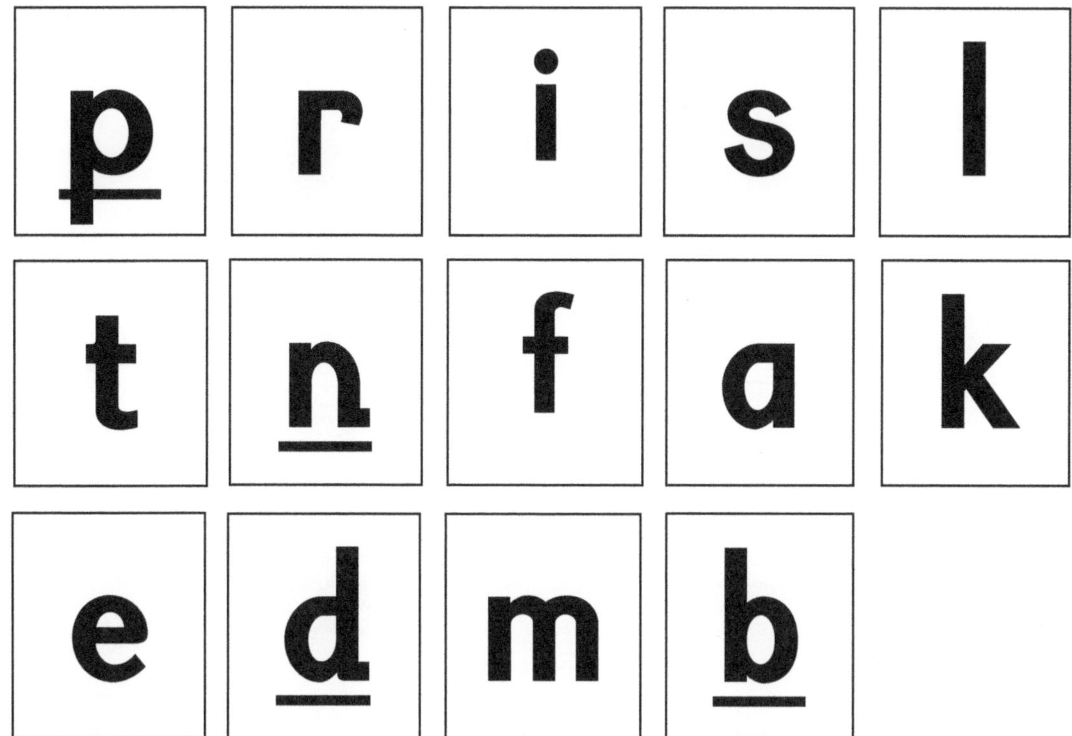

pris > prist > plist > plint > flint > flit > lit > lat > blat > blant > bland > sland > slan > san > sen > sten > stem > stemp > temp > tremp > trem > tren > dren > drenk > renk > rink > brink > brin > prin > pris

Teaching aims: Practice manipulating sounds in CCVCC nonsense words.

Teaching point: Manipulating sounds in nonsense words is a useful activity for older students as they are required to listen to sounds in words they have not seen before and therefore cannot rely on their visual memory. This develops their ability to segment sounds in words.

Teaching guidelines: Ask the student to build the word 'pris', using the cards above. Explain he/she will be building nonsense words. You are going to ask them to change one sound in the word to make a new word. He/she may need to add, take out or change a sound in the word. Ask the student to listen carefully to the new word and change it according to how it sounds. The word may be a real word or a nonsense word. Once the student has built the word, ask him/her to read it. Complete the activity until the student has returned to the original word 'pris'.

Book 5: CCVCC words

Reading captions

1. drips and drops

2. stink from a can

3. a plump skunk

4. a clump of grass

5. hop on a plank

6. frost on a bud

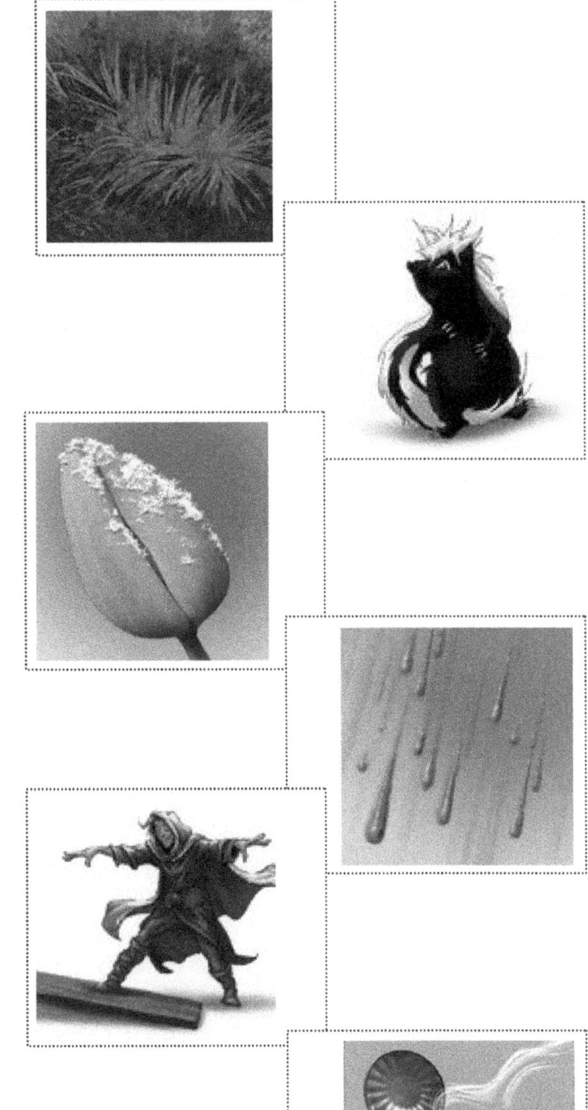

Teaching aims: Reading captions and comprehension

Teaching guidelines: Ask the student to read the captions and draw a line to the matching picture.

Teaching point: When reading high-frequency words, point to the grapheme the student does not yet know and sound it out for the student, e.g. with the word 'the', sound out 'th' and the shwa sound 'uh'.

Book 5: CCVCC words

Writing captions

1. _ _ _ _ _   _ _ _   _ _ _ _ _

2. _ _ _ _ _   _ _ _ _   _   _ _ _

3. _   _ _ _ _ _   _ _ _ _ _

4. _   _ _ _ _ _   of   _ _ _ _

5. _ _ _   _ _   _   _ _ _ _ _

6. _ _ _ _ _   _ _   _   _ _ _

Teaching aims: Writing and spelling captions with CCVCC words

Guidelines: Dictate the captions from the previous page to the student. Ask him/her to listen to the sounds in the words and say them as he/she writes them on the lines.

Book 5: Reading and spelling two-syllable words

Word	✓	Spelling	✓
con/tract	✓	___ /______	
blan/ket		_____ /___	
ex/tinct		__ /______	
splen/did		______ /___	
trust/ed		______ /__	
stunt/man		______ /___	
frost/ed		______ /__	
un/clamp		__ /______	
con/tests		___ /______	

Teaching aims: Reading and spelling words with CCVCC syllables

Teaching guidelines: Fold this sheet along the dotted line. Ask the student to read the words on the left and check off the words she/he has read correctly. Ask the student to turn over the sheet and dictate the words to the student. Ask the student to spell the words by segmenting and sounding out the sounds as she/he writes them on the lines. Ask the student to open the sheet and check off the words she/he has spelled correctly.

Book 5: Comprehension: Spot it!

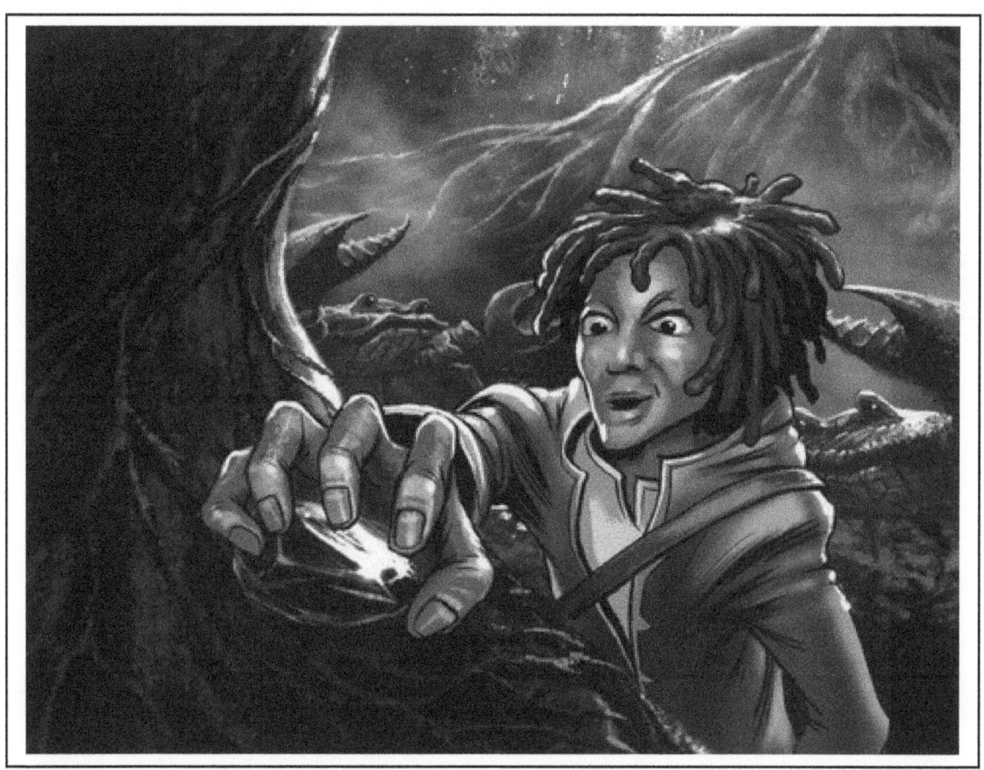

1. Can you spot the black rock?	yes	no
2. Can you spot 3 crabs?	yes	no
3. Can you spot 2 tree trunks?	yes	no
4. Is the black rock on a tree trunk?	yes	no
5. Have the crabs snapped up the black rock?	yes	no
6. Has Finn got the bag on?	yes	no
7. Has Finn grasped the rock with his hand?	yes	no

Teaching guidelines:
This is a comprehension activity. Ask the student to look at the picture and answer the questions. He/she must then circle the words yes or no.

Book 5: Comprehension 2: Sequence the story

1.
2.
3.
4.
5.
6.

The mud crabs crept up and snapped at Finn.

Rat ran on and led Zak and Finn to a bog.

The bog stank. It smelled rank.

Rat got the magic rock from a clump of grass.

Finn spotted the black rock in the twisted tree trunk.

Finn grabbed the rock, but it fell from his hand.

Teaching guidelines:
Cut up the sentences above. Ask the student to read the sentences carefully and sequence them in the order of the story in Book 5, 'Crabs!'. The student then sticks them in the numbered boxes in the correct order.
Words the student may need help with: the, to, a, magic, tree

Book 5: Comprehension 3: Fill in the missing words

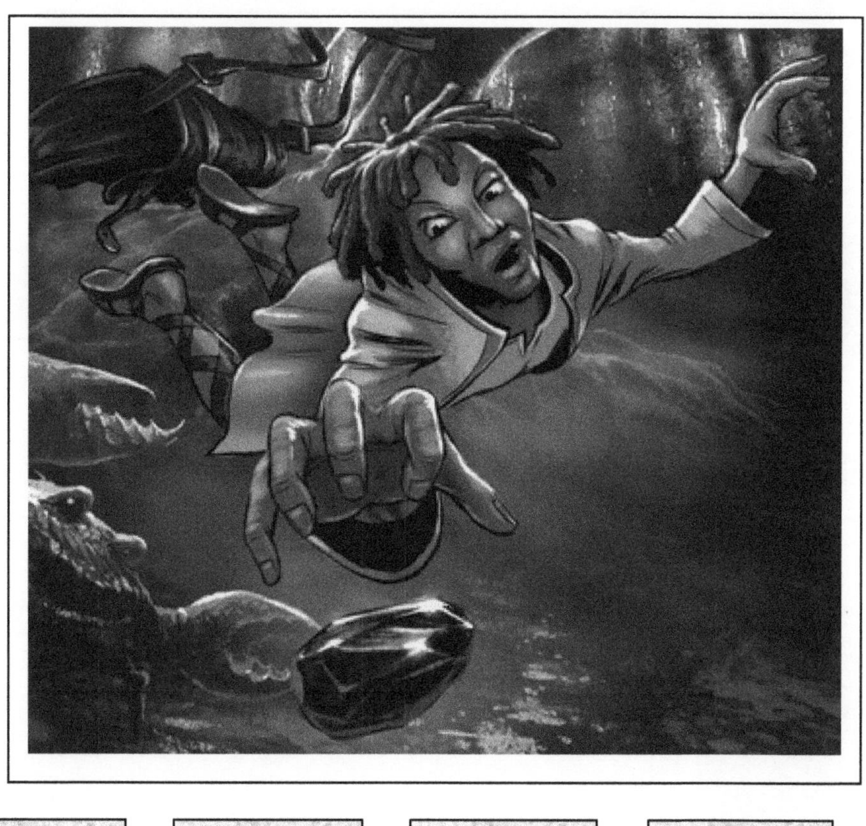

fell	wet	sad	Trust
crabs	slipped	clump	Step

Zak jumped on the _ _ _ _ _ until he got to the grass bank. "_ _ _ _ _ me, Finn! _ _ _ _ on the crabs!" he yelled. Finn stepped onto the _ _ _ crabs, but he _ _ _ _ __ __. The black rock _ _ __ from his hand. Finn was _ _ _. Then Rat got the magic rock from a _ _ _ _ _ of grass.

Teaching guidelines:
Ask the student to read the text and fill in the missing words. He/she should sound out the words as they write them on the lines. He/she can cross out the words in the boxes above as they use them in the text.

Book 5: Writing frame

bog stank smelled
rank sinking sand

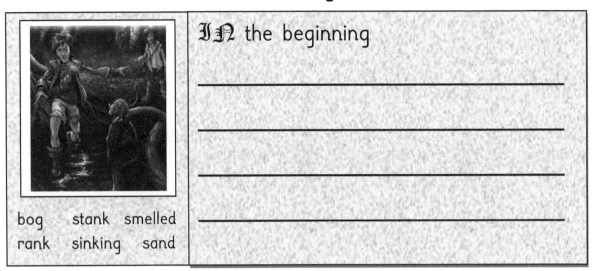

IN the beginning

____

____

____

____

crabs snap black
rock tree trunk

IN the middle

____

____

____

____

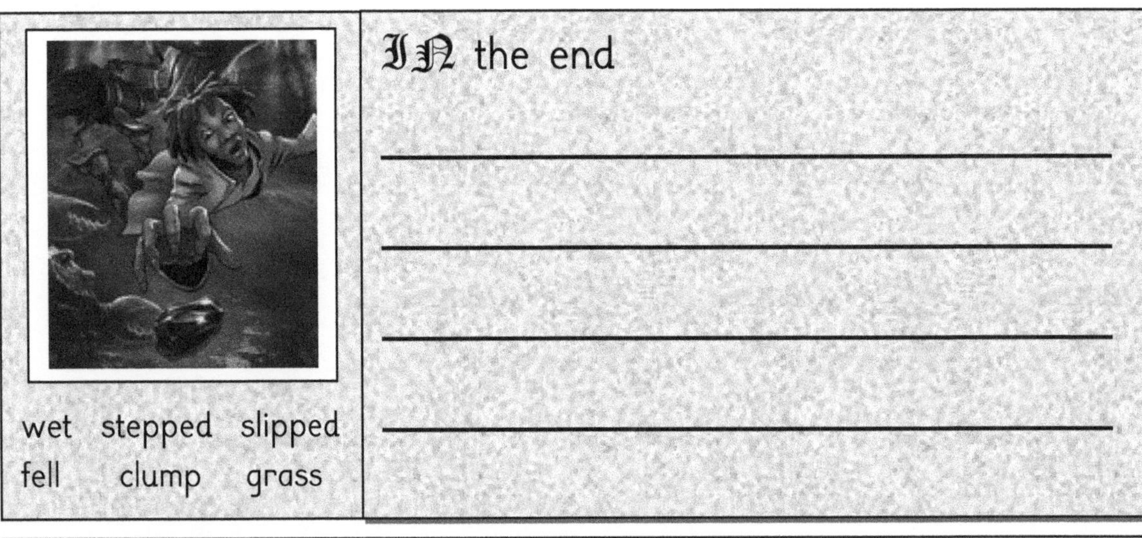

wet stepped slipped
fell clump grass

IN the end

____

____

____

____

Teaching guidelines: Above is a writing frame to help the student to sequence the story. Some words are provided under the images to support spelling.

Book 5: Vocabulary

New words in Book 5:
slumped – fell heavily
grand – great or splendid!
prodded – poked or jabbed
bog – an area of wet spongy ground
flapped – panicked
dank – unpleasantly damp and chilly
clump – a group of plants growing in one place

Finn slept on. Zak	stank. It smelled rank.
The lads slumped	in a clump of grass.
The rock was hidden	and grand.
The crabs lived in	next to a tree trunk.
The bog	began to sink.
Finn yelled when he	prodded him.
The trees were big	a cold and dank bog.

Teaching guidelines:
This activity includes new vocabulary introduced in Book 5, 'Crabs!'. It encourages the student to think about the meaning of the new words and to use them to construct a complete sentence. Cut the sentences into strips and cut along the dotted line. Ask the student to match the two parts of the sentence so that they make sense. The student may need a reminder of what the words mean.

Book 5: Punctuation activity

Finn grasped the rock in his hand the mud crabs crept up to his legs

finn stepped on the wet crabs he slipped the rock fell from his hand

finn was sad he had lost the rock in the bog then rat got it from a clump of grass

Did you spot?

8 missing full stops

8 missing capital letters

Book 5: Stepping stones game: CCVCC

START

flags

drank

swift

clump

blond

tramp

plump

skunk

stand

drips

slots

slump

plank

grand

trump

crisp

trend

frost

grunt

twins

trust

FINISH

bland

stump

steps

prank

print

clamp

brand

This game is for 1–4 players. Play with counters and die. This sheet may be photocopied by the purchaser.

Book 6: Crunch!

Questions for discussion

Chapter 1

1. What is a 'hatchet'? (p. 3)
2. What did Finn do after he ate his cheese? (p. 4)

Chapter 2

1. What is a 'mud flat'? (p. 5)

Chapter 3

1. Where did Finn find the green gem? (p. 7)
2. How did Finn try to get the gem out of the rock? (p. 8)
3. What made the dragon in the rock stir? (p. 9)

Chapter 4

1. What are 'talons'? (p. 11)
2. Why do you think the rock dragon crumbled to dust? (p. 12)

Teaching guidelines:
These questions can be discussed after reading the text. They will help develop speaking and listening skills, comprehension and vocabulary.

Book 6: Word-building with 'ch'

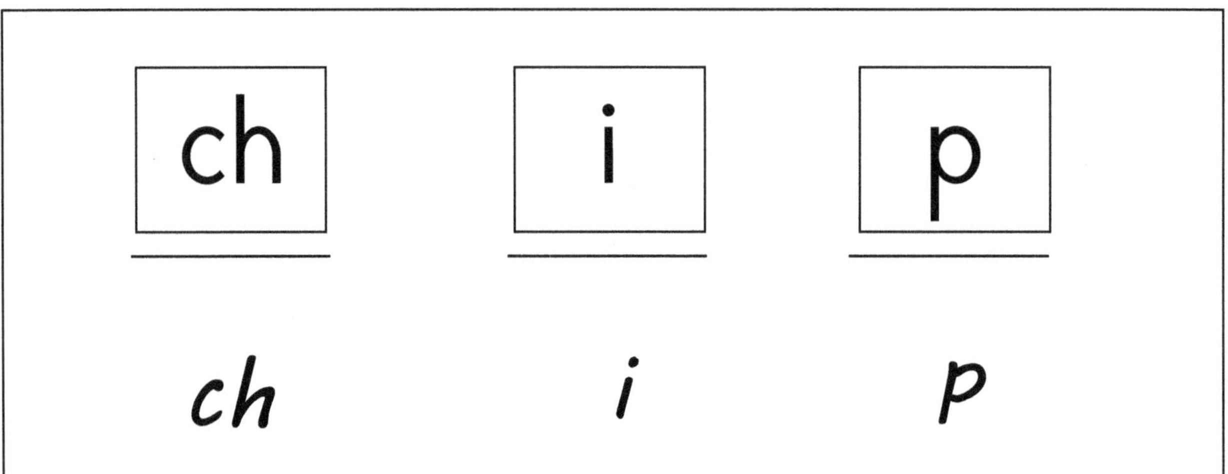

Teaching aims:

- Learn the sound 'ch' and the corresponding spellings: <ch> and <tch>
- Segment and blend words with the sound 'ch'

Teacher guidelines:

Use a white board on which three lines have been drawn. Make cards for the spellings <ch> and <tch>. Add them to the cards with the letters of the alphabet from previous levels.

1. **Teach word-building with the spelling<ch>**

First teach the spelling <ch>. Select a word from the list below. Use only the letters needed to build that word and jumble them up. Ask the student to build that word by listening to the sounds in the word and segmenting all the sounds in the word, one at a time. The student places each card on the appropriate line once he/she has segmented the word. Ask the student to read the word he/she has built. Ask the student to write the word under the lines, saying the sounds as he/she does. Draw more lines for longer words.

2. **Teach word-building with the spelling <tch>**

Follow the steps above with the spelling <tch>.

Word list for word-building, reading and spelling:

<ch>: chat, chess, chill, chin, chop, chum, chunk, chimp, much, such, inch, rich, bench, lunch
<tch>: fetch, patch, batch, hutch, catch, glitch, stitch, hatch, snitch, pitch, ditch, clutch, Dutch

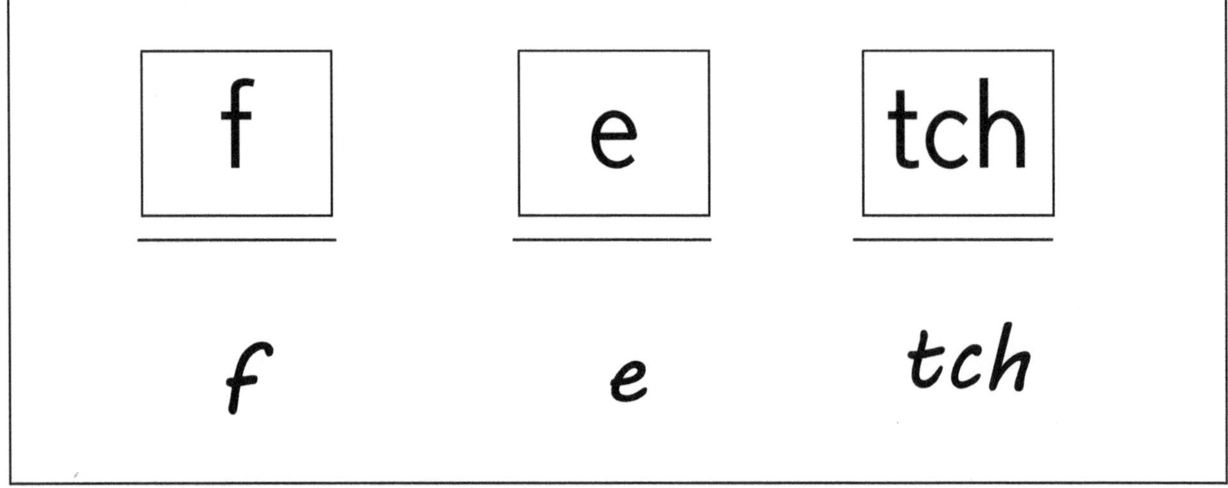

Book 6: Reading and spelling 'ch'

Word		Spelling	
chip	✓	___ ___ ___	
chess		___ ___ ___	
chin		___ ___ ___	
much		___ ___ ___	
bench		___ ___ ___ ___	
lunch		___ ___ ___ ___	
catch		___ ___ ___	
ditch		___ ___ ___	
hutch		___ ___ ___	

Teaching aims: Reading and spelling words with the spellings <ch> and <tch> for the sound 'ch'

Teaching guidelines: Fold this sheet along the dotted line. Ask the student to read the words on the left and check off the words she/he has read correctly. Ask the student to turn over the sheet and dictate the words to the student. Ask the student to spell the words by segmenting and sounding out the sounds as she/he writes them on the lines. Ask the student to open the sheet and check off the words she/he has spelled correctly.

Book 6: <ch> and <tch> spellings

Reading accuracy

chops
chums
chips

chit
chin
chill

chimp
chomp
champ

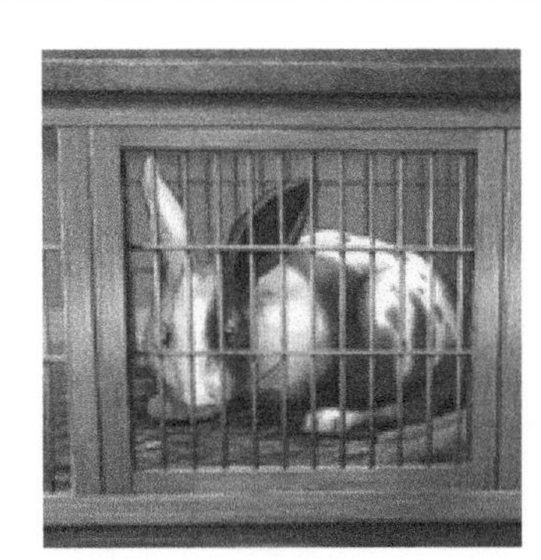

pitch
Dutch
hutch

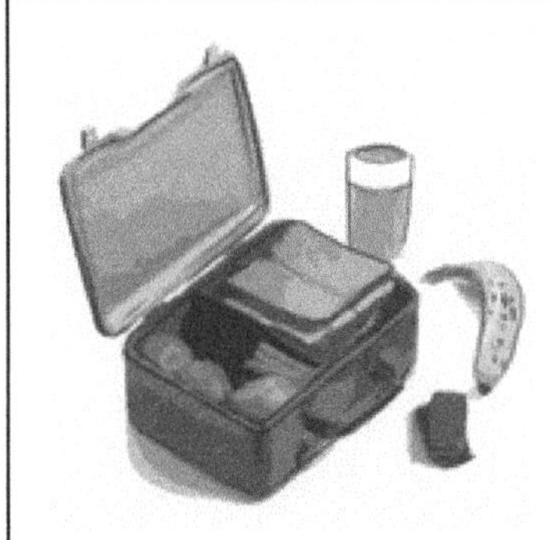

hunch
lunch
chunk

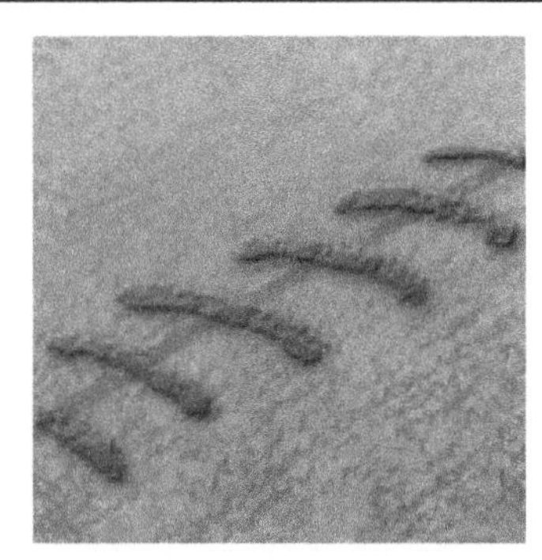

stitch
pitch
ditch

Teaching aims: Reading accuracy

Teaching guidelines: Ask the student to read the words in each box and circle the word that matches the picture.

Book 6: <ch> nonsense words

Full circle game: playing with sounds

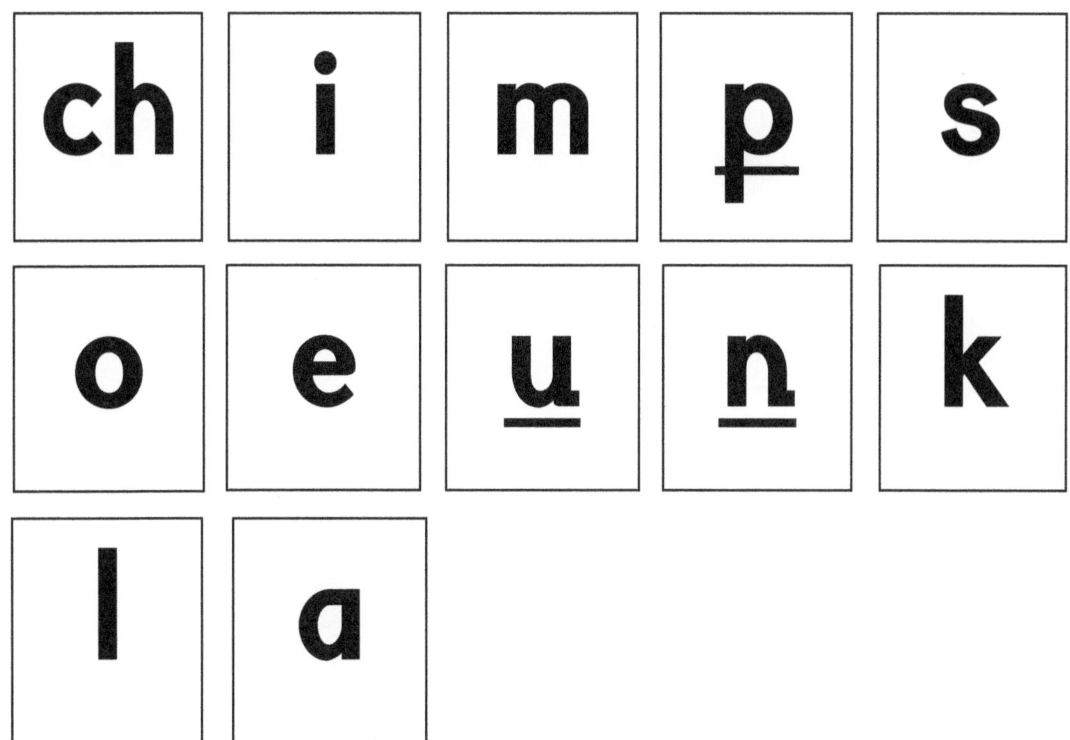

chim > chimp > chimps > chips > ips > ups > chups > cheps > chens > chuns > chun > chunk > chank > ank > an > en > men > ment > lent > lench > linch > pinch > inch > onch > on > chon > chom > chim

Teaching aims: Practice manipulating sounds 'ch' with the spelling <ch> in nonsense words.

Teaching point: Manipulating sounds in nonsense words is a useful activity for older students as they are required to listen to sounds in words they have not seen before and therefore cannot rely on their visual memory. This develops their ability to segment sounds in words.

Teaching guidelines: Ask the student to build the word 'chim', using the cards above. Explain he/she will be building nonsense words. You are going to ask them to change one sound in the word to make a new word. He/she may need to add, take out or change a sound in the word. Ask the student to listen carefully to the new word and change it according to how it sounds. The word may be a real word or a nonsense word. Once the student has built the word, ask him/her to read it. Complete the activity until the student has returned to the original word 'chim'.

Book 6: <ch> and <tch> spellings

Reading captions

1. a pet in a hutch

2. Catch it!

3. a big chimp

4. chips in a bag

5. Chop the logs.

6. lunch in a box

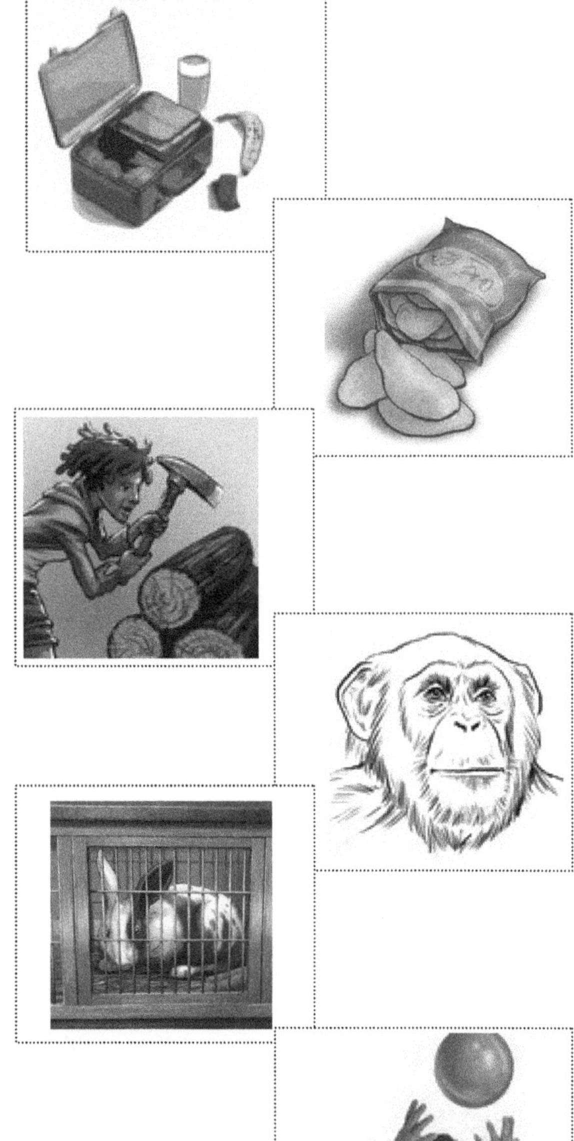

Teaching aims: Reading captions and comprehension

Teaching guidelines: Ask the student to read the captions and draw a line to the matching picture.

Teaching point: When reading high-frequency words, point to the grapheme the student does not yet know and sound it out for the student, e.g. with the word 'the', sound out 'th' and the shwa sound 'uh'.

Book 6: <ch> and <tch>

Writing captions

1. __ ___ __ __ __ ___ ____

2. ___ ____ __!

3. __ ___ ____

4. ____ __ __ __

5. ___ the ____.

6. ____ __ __ ___

Teaching aims: Writing and spelling captions with <ch> and <tch>

Guidelines: Dictate the captions from the previous page to the student. Ask him/her to listen to the sounds in the words and say them as he/she writes them on the lines.

Book 6: Reading and spelling two-syllable words

Word	✓	Spelling	✓
chip/munk	✓	_ _ _/_ _ _ _	
lunch/box		_ _ _ _/_ _ _	
chick/en		_ _ _/_ _	
chin/strap		_ _ _/_ _ _ _ _	
rich/ness		_ _ _/_ _ _	
ost/rich		_ _ _/_ _ _	
chest/nut		_ _ _ _/_ _ _	
match/box		_ _ _/_ _ _	
hatch/et		_ _ _/_ _	

Teaching aims: Reading and spelling words with <ch and tch> spellings

Teaching guidelines: Fold this sheet along the dotted line. Ask the student to read the words on the left and check off the words she/he has read correctly. Ask the student to turn over the sheet and dictate the words to the student. Ask the student to spell the words by segmenting and sounding out the sounds as she/he writes them on the lines. Ask the student to open the sheet and check off the words she/he has spelled correctly.

Book 6: Comprehension: Spot it!

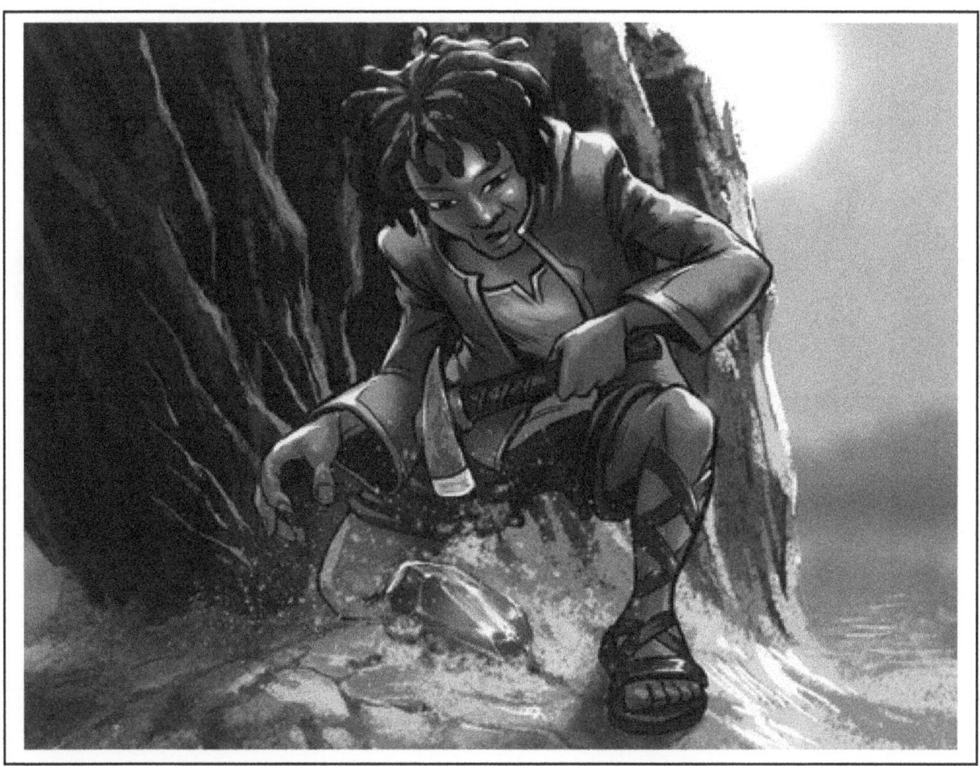

1. Is the sun setting?	yes	no
2. Can you spot the cracked mud?	yes	no
3. Can you spot the gem?	yes	no
4. Has Zak got the hatchet?	yes	no
5. Has Finn got the hatchet in his left hand?	yes	no
6. Is Finn chipping at the rock?	yes	no
7. Can you spot the dragon's talons?	yes	no

Teaching guidelines:
This is a comprehension activity. Ask the student to look at the picture and answer the questions. He/she must then circle the words yes or no.

Book 6: Comprehension 2: Sequence the story

1.
2.
3.
4.
5.
6.

Finn spotted the gem. It was attached to a big rock.

Zak, Finn and Rat ran to a mud flat.

Finn held the rock. The rock dragon crumbled to dust.

A rock dragon hatched from the rock.

Finn chipped at the rock with the hatchet.

The dragon stretched his talons to catch Finn.

Teaching guidelines:
Cut up the sentences above. Ask the student to read the sentences carefully and sequence them in the order of the story in Book 6, 'Crunch!'. The student then sticks them in the numbered boxes in the correct order.
Words the student may need help with: the, gem, was, to, a, crumbled, with, his

Book 6: Comprehension 3: Fill in the missing words

talons	snatch	attached	began
twitch	catch	dragon	chipped

The gem was _ __ _ __ __ to the rock. Finn __ _ __ __ at the rock. The dragon _ _ _ _ _ to _ _ _ __. Finn ran to _ _ _ __ the gem. The dragon stretched his _ _ _ _ _ _ to _ _ __ him. Just as Finn got the gem, the _ _ _ _ _ _ crumbled to dust.

Teaching guidelines:
Ask the student to read the text and fill in the missing words. He/she should sound out the words as they write them on the lines. He/she can cross out the words in the boxes above as they use them in the text.

Book 6: Writing frame

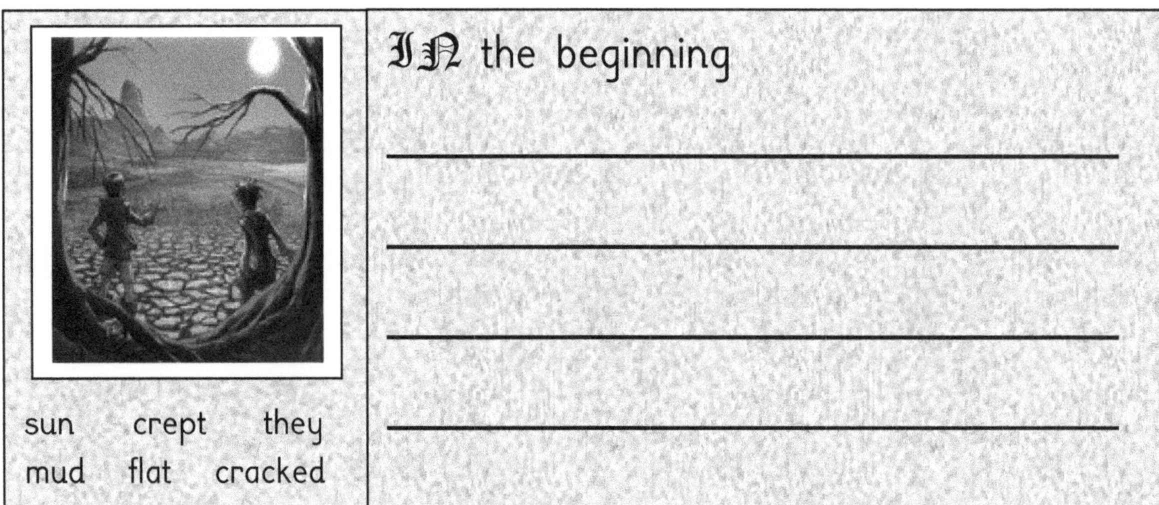

IN the beginning
sun crept they
mud flat cracked

IN the middle

Finn chipped gem
with hatchet rock

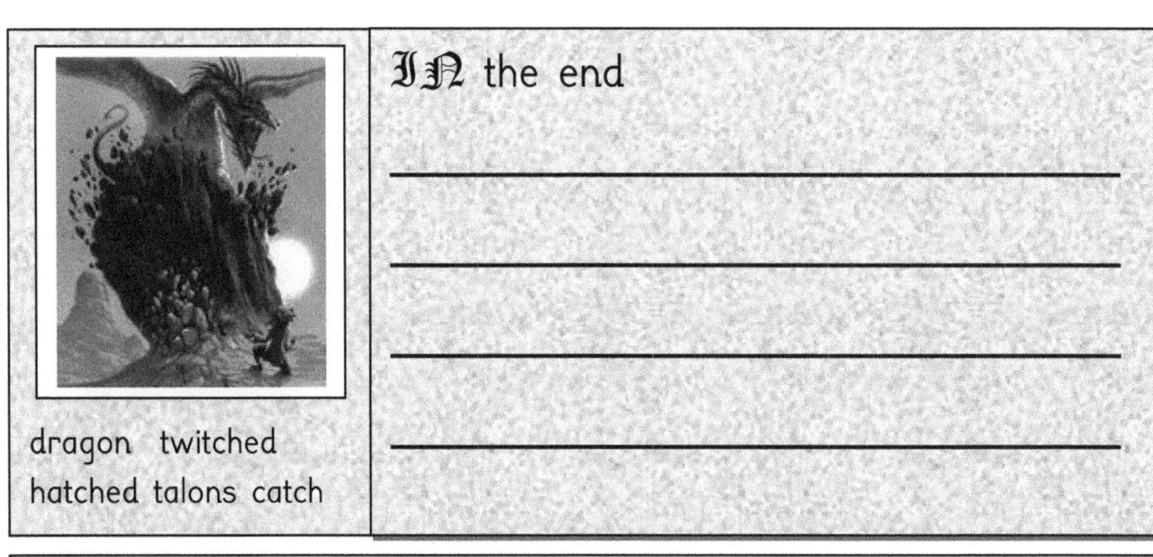

IN the end
dragon twitched
hatched talons catch

Teaching guidelines: Above is a writing frame to help the student to sequence the story. Some words are provided under the images to support spelling.

Book 6: Vocabulary

New words in Book 6:
hatchet – a small axe
belched – to let wind out of your mouth noisily
mud flat – low muddy land that is covered at high tide and exposed at low tide
gem – a precious stone
chipped – knocked small pieces off
talons – strong claws

A hatchet is a	its talons to catch Finn.
The dragon stretched	attached to the rock.
Finn had a chunk of	small axe.
The dragon hatched	cheese. Then he belched.
Finn chipped at the	flat was cracked.
The mud on the mud	from the rock.
Finn saw the gem	rock with the hatchet.

Teaching guidelines:
This activity includes new vocabulary introduced in Book 6, 'Crunch!'. It encourages the student to think about the meaning of the new words and to use them to construct a complete sentence. Cut the sentences into strips and cut along the dotted line. Ask the student to match the two parts of the sentence so that they make sense. The student may need a reminder of what the words mean.

Book 6: Punctuation activity

Finn let rat run up his chest and onto his chin

zak and finn went to fetch branches from the forest finn chopped them up with his hatchet

finn and zak chatted by the fire they munched on chunks of cheese finn belched

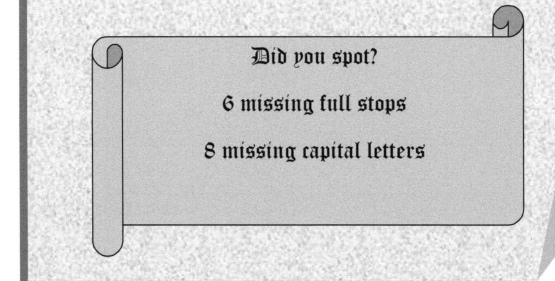

Did you spot?

6 missing full stops

8 missing capital letters

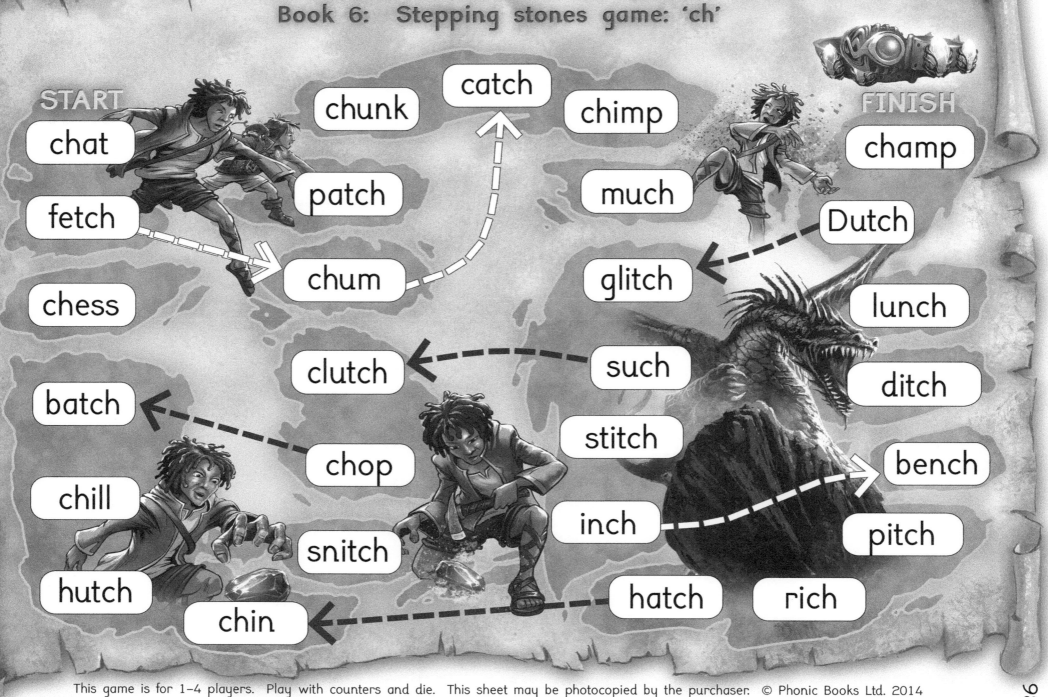

Book 6: Stepping stones game: 'ch'

START

chat

fetch

chess

batch

chill

hutch

chunk

patch

chum

clutch

chop

snitch

chin

catch

chimp

much

glitch

such

stitch

inch

hatch

rich

pitch

bench

ditch

lunch

Dutch

champ

FINISH

This game is for 1–4 players. Play with counters and die. This sheet may be photocopied by the purchaser.

Book 7: Hush!

Questions for discussion

Chapter 1

1. Describe what a lush forest is like. (p. 2)
2. Why was there an odd hush in the village? (p. 3)

Chapter 2

1. Who do you think trapped Zak and Finn in the mesh? (p. 5)
2. How did they get out of the mesh? (p. 6)

Chapter 3

1. How did Zak find the gray rock? (p. 8)
2. Why do you think the magic rock was in the chest? (p. 8)
3. Why do you think the goblins surrounded Zak? (p. 9)

Chapter 4

1. How do you think Zak felt when the goblins attacked him? (p. 11)
2. How does the story end? (p. 12)

Teaching guidelines:
These questions can be discussed after reading the text. They will help develop speaking and listening skills, comprehension and vocabulary.

Book 7: Word-building with 'sh'

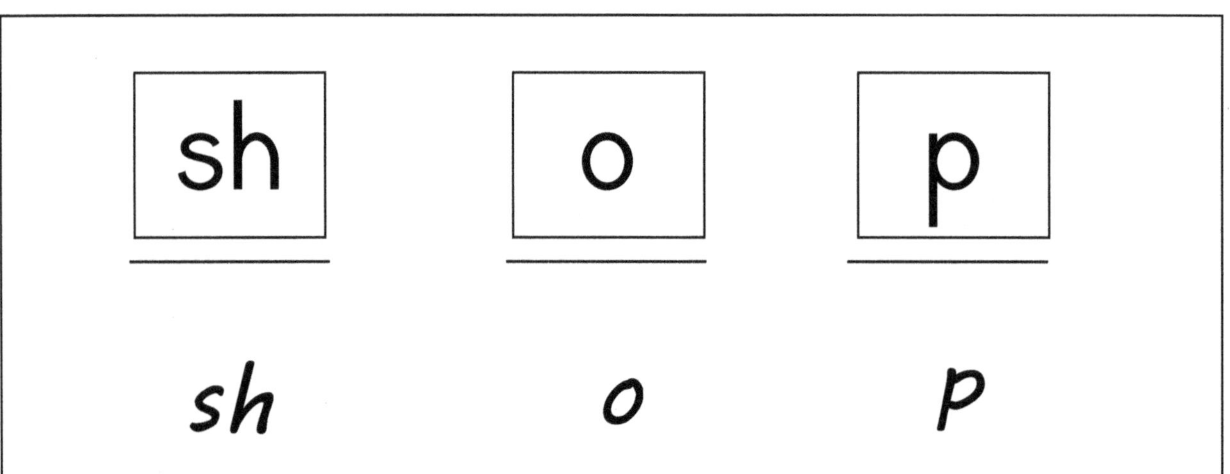

Teaching aims:

- learn the sound 'sh' and the corresponding spelling <sh>
- be able to segment and blend words with 'sh'

Teacher guidelines:
Use a white board on which three lines have been drawn. Make a card for the spelling <sh>. Add it to the cards with the letters of the alphabet from previous levels.

Teach word-building with the spelling <sh>
Select a word from the list below. Use only the letters needed to build that word and jumble them up. Ask the student to build that word by listening to the sounds in the word and segmenting all the sounds in the word, one at a time. The student then places each card on the appropriate line once he/she has segmented the word. Ask the student to read the word he/she has built. Ask the student to write the word under the lines, saying the sounds as he/she does. Draw more lines for longer words.

Word list for word-building, reading and spelling:
Shop, shed, shin, shut, ship, shall, shell, shift, shred, shot, rush, gash, wish, dash, fish, dish, posh, hush, bash, crash, smash, splash, clash, brash, shrub, shrug, brush, shelf

Book 7: Reading and spelling 'sh'

Word	✓	Spelling	✓
shop	✓	___ ___ ___	
shell		___ ___ ___	
shut		___ ___ ___	
wish		___ ___ ___	
hush		___ ___ ___	
dash		___ ___ ___	
brush		___ ___ ___ ___	
smash		___ ___ ___ ___	
shrug		___ ___ ___ ___	

Teaching aims: Reading and spelling words with 'sh'

Teaching guidelines: Fold this sheet along the dotted line. Ask the student to read the words on the left and check off the words she/he has read correctly. Ask the student to turn over the sheet and dictate the words to the student. Ask the student to spell the words by segmenting and sounding out the sounds as she/he writes them on the lines. Ask the student to open the sheet and check off the words she/he has spelled correctly.

Book 7: 'sh'

Reading accuracy

ship
shin
shun

shrub
crush
brush

shot
shop
shut

shelf
shank
shrimp

hush
cash
mash

fish
wish
slush

Teaching aims: Reading accuracy

Teaching guidelines: Ask the student to read the words in each box and circle the word that matches the picture.

Book 7: 'sh' nonsense words

Full circle game: playing with sounds

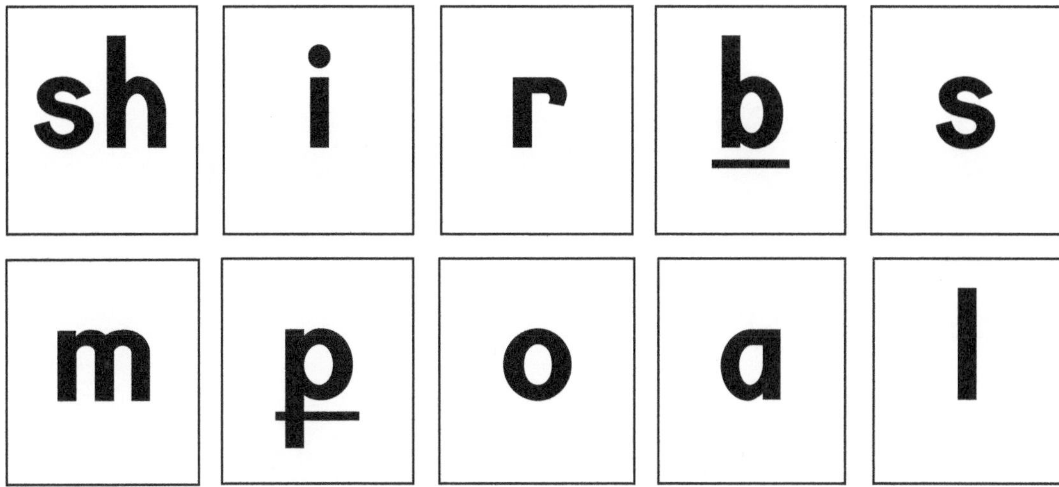

shib > shrib > shribs > shrims > shrimps > shimps> shimp > shim > im > ish > ash> pash > plash > splash > splosh > plosh > losh > lish > lib > shib

Teaching aims: Practice manipulating sounds 'sh' in nonsense words.

Teaching point: Manipulating sounds in nonsense words is a useful activity for older students as they are required to listen to sounds in words they have not seen before and therefore cannot rely on their visual memory. This develops their ability to segment sounds in words.

Teaching guidelines: Ask the student to build the word 'shib', using the cards above. Explain he/she will be building nonsense words. You are going to ask them to change one sound in the word to make a new word. He/she may need to add, take out or change a sound in the word. Ask the student to listen carefully to the new word and change it according to how it sounds. The word may be a real word or a nonsense word. Once the student has built the word, ask him/her to read it. Complete the activity until the student has returned to the original word 'shib'.

Book 7: 'sh'

Reading captions

1. a big splash

2. junk on a shelf

3. a fish tank

4. shell in the sand

5. gash on a shin

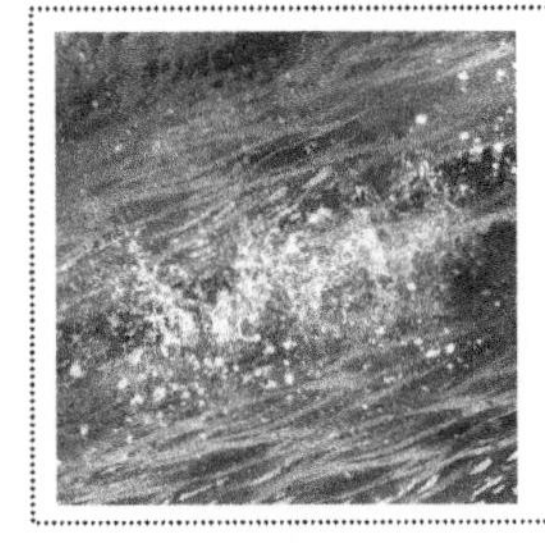

6. ship on a pond

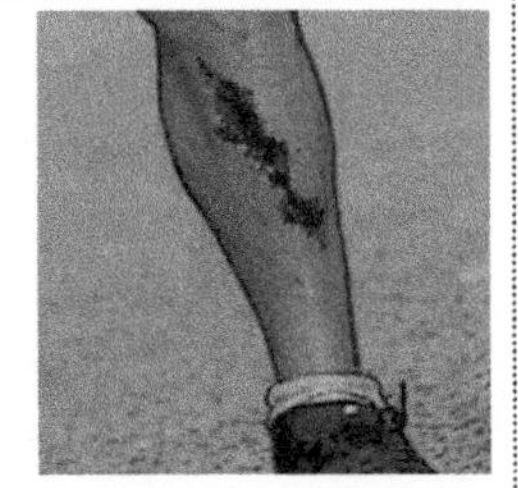

Teaching aims: Reading captions and comprehension

Teaching guidelines: Ask the student to read the captions and draw a line to the matching picture.

Teaching point: When reading high-frequency words, point to the grapheme the student does not yet know and sound it out for the student, e.g. with the word 'the', sound out 'th' and the shwa sound 'uh'.

Book 7: 'sh'

Writing captions

1. __ ___ _____

2. ____ __ _ ____

3. _ ___ ____

4. ___ __ <u>th</u>e ____

5. ___ __ _ ___

6. ___ __ _ ____

Teaching aims: Writing and spelling captions with 'sh'

Guidelines: Dictate the captions from the previous page to the student. Ask him/her to listen to the sounds in the words and say them as he/she writes them on the lines.

Book 7: Reading and spelling two-syllable words

shell/fish	✓	______/____	
egg/shell		___/______	
ship/ment		____/_____	
dish/rag		_____/___	
pol/ish		___/___	
fin/ish		___/___	
Brit/ish		____/___	
rad/ish		___/___	
flag/ship		____/____	

Teaching aims: Reading and spelling words with 'sh'

Teaching guidelines: Fold this sheet along the dotted line. Ask the student to read the words on the left and check off the words she/he has read correctly. Ask the student to turn over the sheet and dictate the words to the student. Ask the student to spell the words by segmenting and sounding out the sounds as she/he writes them on the lines. Ask the student to open the sheet and check off the words she/he has spelled correctly.

Book 7: Comprehension: Spot it!

1. Can you spot the lush forest?	yes	no
2. Can you spot a mob of goblins?	yes	no
3. Can you spot the chest?	yes	no
4. Is the magic rock in the chest?	yes	no
5. Have the goblins got the magic rock?	yes	no
6. Can you spot the mesh?	yes	no
7. Is the magic rock in Zak's hand?	yes	no

Teaching guidelines:
This is a comprehension activity. Ask the student to look at the picture and answer the questions. He/she must then circle the words yes or no.

Book 7: Comprehension 2: Sequence the story

1.
2.
3.
4.
5.
6.

Zak held the rock. The goblins rushed at him.

The goblins trapped Zak and Finn in a mesh.

Zak ran and crashed into a chest with the magic rock.

Finn crashed into the goblins and they fled.

Zak and Finn ran to a village with grass huts.

Rat nipped the mesh into shreds.

Teaching guidelines:
Cut up the sentences above. Ask the student to read the sentences carefully and sequence them in the order of the story in Book 7, 'Hush!'. The student then sticks them in the numbered boxes in the correct order.
Words the student may need help with: the, rock, a, into, with, magic, they, to, village

Book 7: Comprehension 3: Fill in the missing words

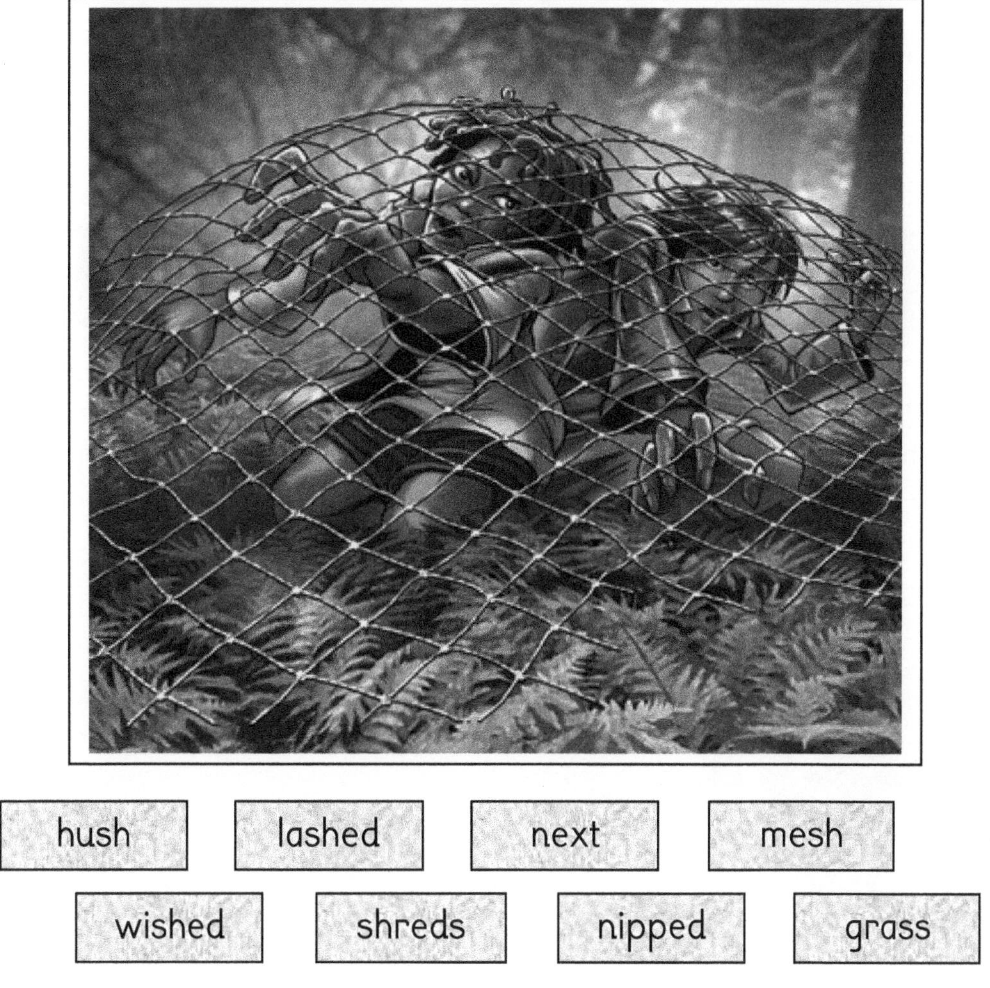

hush	lashed	next	mesh
wished	shreds	nipped	grass

Zak and Finn ran to a village with _ _ _ __ huts.

There was an odd _ _ __. Zak _ _ __ __ he was back with Grandpa. The _ _ _ _ day, the goblins trapped them in a _ _ __.

Finn _ _ __ __ out. Rat _ _ __ __ the mesh. He bit the mesh into __ _ _ _ _.

Teaching guidelines:
Ask the student to read the text and fill in the missing words. He/she should sound out the words as they write them on the lines. He/she can cross out the words in the boxes above as they use them in the text.

Book 7: Writing frame

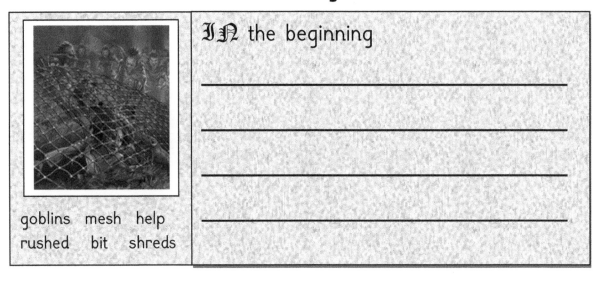

IN the beginning

goblins mesh help
rushed bit shreds

IN the middle

crashed chest shut
snapped shuffle mob

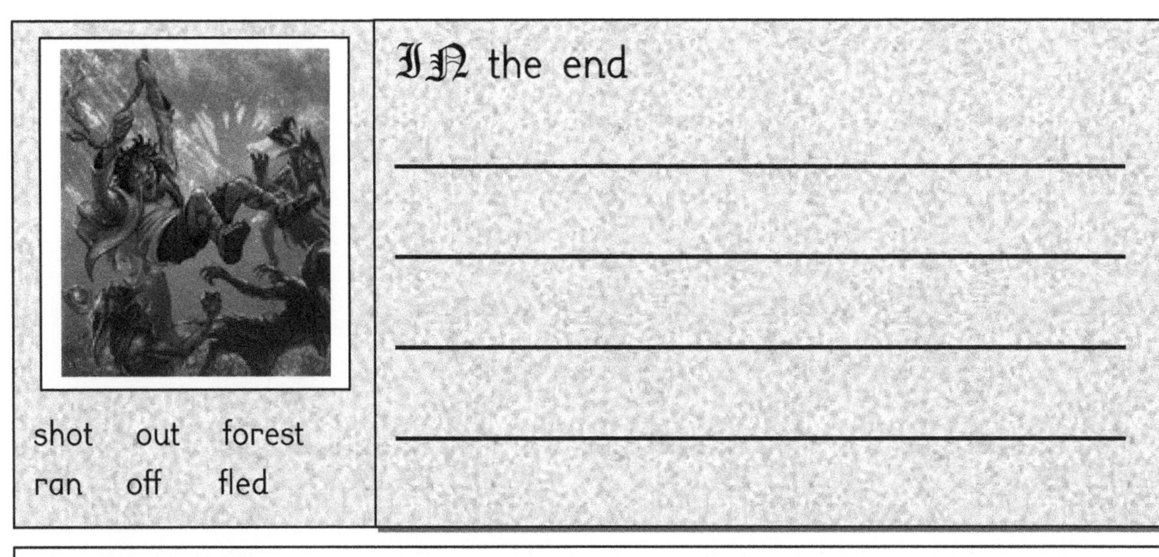

IN the end
shot out forest
ran off fled

Teaching guidelines: Above is a writing frame to help the student to sequence the story. Some words are provided under the images to support spelling.

Book 7: Vocabulary

New words in Book 7:
lush – growing abundantly
hush – silence, quiet
mesh – material like a net
lashed out – hit out angrily
shreds – cuts into little pieces
goblins – evil or mischievous fairy in stories
mob – a large, disorderly crowd

They ran into	hush in the village.
There was on odd	rushed at Zak.
Goblins trapped	into shreds.
Finn was angry and	Zak and Finn in a mesh.
The goblins lived in	a lush forest.
Rat bit the mesh	the village of grass huts.
A mob of goblins	he lashed out.

Teaching guidelines:
This activity includes new vocabulary introduced in Book 7, 'Hush!'. It encourages the student to think about the meaning of the new words and to use them to construct a complete sentence. Cut the sentences into strips and cut along the dotted line. Ask the student to match the two parts of the sentence so that they make sense. The student may need a reminder of what the words mean.

Book 7: Punctuation activity

The lads dashed into the forest they ran as fast as the wind

zak crashed into a chest the lid flipped up the magic rock was in the chest

zak got the rock from the chest the goblins got cross they rushed at him

Did you spot?

8 missing full stops

7 missing capital letters

Book 7: Stepping stones game: 'sh'

START

shop

shed

shin

shut

ship

shall

dash

wish

gash

rush

shot

shred

shift

posh

fish

dish

posh

hush

bash

crash

smash

FINISH

shrug

shelf

brush

shrub

brash

clash

splash

This game is for 1–4 players. Play with counters and die. This sheet may be photocopied by the purchaser.

Book 8: The Sixth Rock

Questions for discussion

Chapter 1

1. How do you know that Finn was enjoying the quest? (p. 1)
2. How can we know that Zak is happy that Finn was coming on the quest? (p. 1)

Chapter 2

1. What did the tramp look like? (p. 3)
2. What did the tramp have hidden in his clothes? (p. 4)
3. What was the tramp going to do with the magic rocks? (p. 5)

Chapter 3

1. What did Zak discover when he woke up? (p. 6)
2. Why was Zak frantic? (p. 9)
3. Why didn't the tramp notice Rat? (p. 10)

Chapter 4

1. Why did the gems fall out of the bag? (p. 11)
2. Why does Finn think they should thank Rat? (p. 12)

Teaching guidelines:
These questions can be discussed after reading the text. They will help develop speaking and listening skills, comprehension and vocabulary.

Book 8: Word-building with <th>

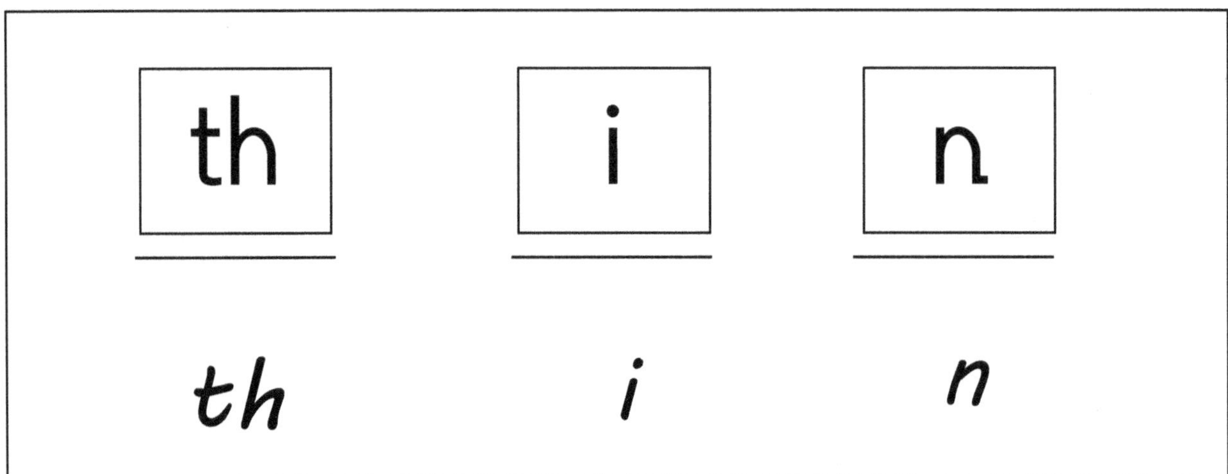

Teaching aims:

- Learn the two sounds for the spelling <th>
- Segement and blend words with the spelling <th>

Teacher guidelines:

Use a white board on which three lines have been drawn. Make a card for the spelling <th>. Add it to the cards with the letters of the alphabet from previous levels.

Teach word-building with the spelling <th>

Teach the spelling <th>. Explain that it can represent two different sounds: 'th' as in 'thin' and 'th' as in 'this'. Select a word from the list below. Use only the letters needed to build that word and jumble them up. Ask the student to build that word by listening to the sounds in the word and segmenting all the sounds in the word, one at a time. The student then places each card on the appropriate line once he/she has segmented the word. Ask the student to read the word he/she has built. Ask the student to write the word under the lines, saying the sounds as he/she does. Draw more lines for longer words.

Word list for word-building, reading and spelling:

'th' as in 'thin': thin, fifth, thrill, thank, think, moth, broth, thud, throb, froth, depth, cloth, width
'th' as in 'this': this, that, then, them, thus, with

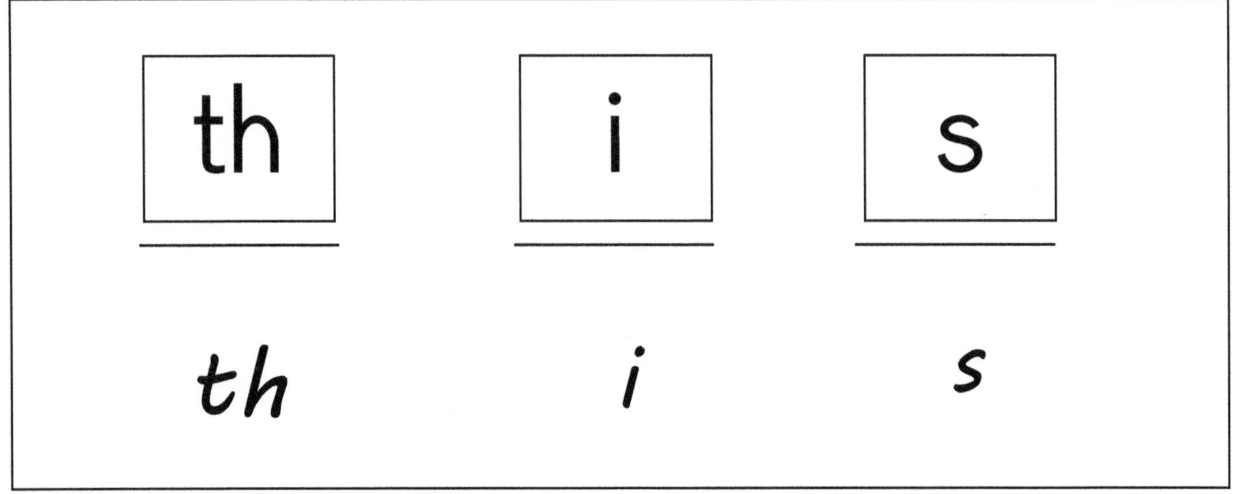

Book 8: Reading and spelling <th>

thin	✓	___ __ __	
thank		___ __ __ __	
think		___ __ __ __	
moth		__ __ ___	
them		___ __ __	
with		__ __ ___	
this		___ __ __	
that		___ __ __	
then		___ __ __	

Teaching aims: Reading and spelling words with spelling <th>

Teaching guidelines: Fold this sheet along the dotted line. Ask the student to read the words on the left and check off the words she/he has read correctly. Ask the student to turn over the sheet and dictate the words to the student. Ask the student to spell the words by segmenting and sounding out the sounds as she/he writes them on the lines. Ask the student to open the sheet and check off the words she/he has spelled correctly.

Book 8: <th> spelling

Reading accuracy

with
this
thin

that
cloth
than

thrush
broth
throb

thank
width
think

then
them
moth

fifth
seventh
tenth

Teaching aims: Reading accuracy

Teaching guidelines: Ask the student to read the words in each box and circle the word that matches the picture.

Book 8: 'th' (non-voiced) nonsense words

Full circle game: playing with sounds

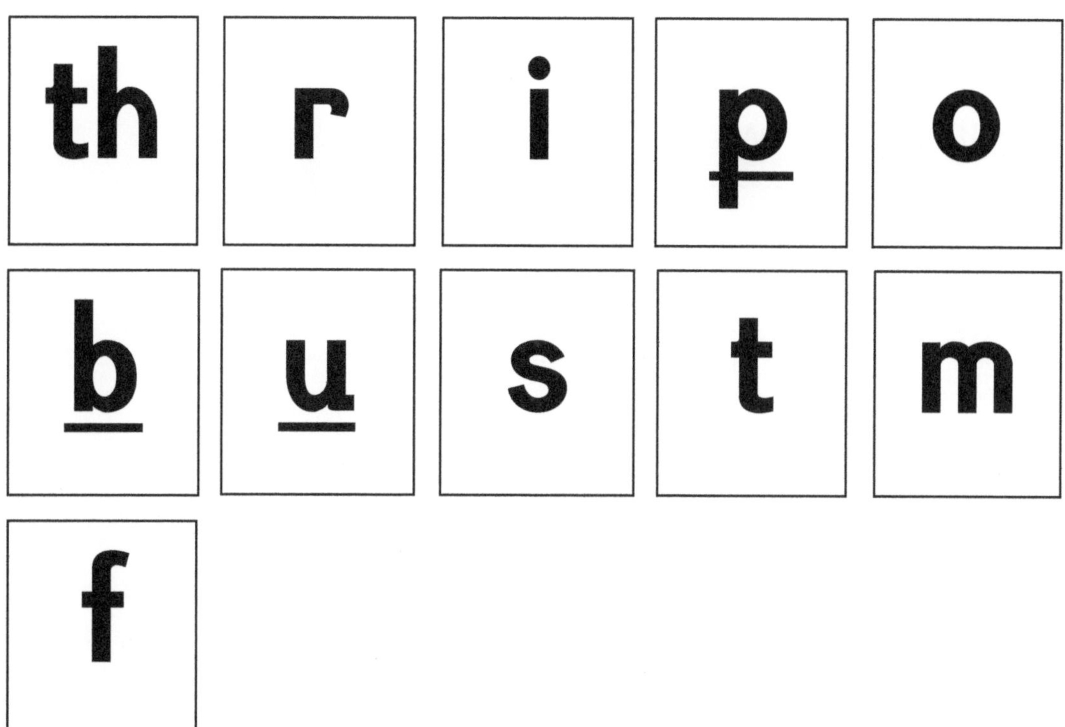

thip > thrip > throp > throb > thrub > thrus > thrust > throst > throt > throm > thom > thomp > thump > ump > omp > op > oth > foth > froth > frith > rith > rip > thip

Teaching aims: Practice manipulating sounds 'th' in nonsense words.

Teaching point: Manipulating sounds in nonsense words is a useful activity for older students as they are required to listen to sounds in words they have not seen before and therefore cannot rely on their visual memory. This develops their ability to segment sounds in words.

Teaching guidelines: Ask the student to build the word 'thip', using the cards above. Explain he/she will be building nonsense words. You are going to ask them to change one sound in the word to make a new word. He/she may need to add, take out or change a sound in the word. Ask the student to listen carefully to the new word and change it according to how it sounds. The word may be a real word or a nonsense word. Once the student has built the word, ask him/her to read it. Complete the activity until the student has returned

Book 8: <th>

Reading captions

1. Think of a wish.

2. This is a map.

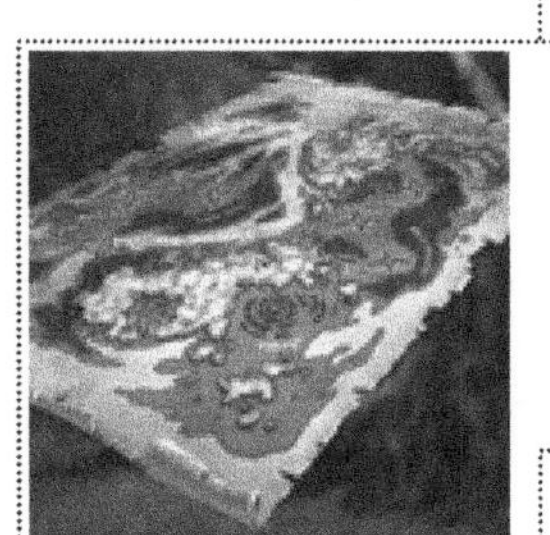

3. the fifth man

4. That is a shed.

5. a thin man

6. moth on a lamp

Teaching aims: Reading captions and comprehension

Teaching guidelines: Ask the student to read the captions and draw a line to the matching picture.

Teaching point: When reading high-frequency words, point to the grapheme the student does not yet know and sound it out for the student, e.g. with the word 'the', sound out 'th' and the shwa sound 'uh'.

Book 8: <th>

Writing captions

1. ___ __ __ __ of __ __ __ ___.

2. ___ __ __ __ __ __ __ __ __.

3. ___ __ __ __ __ ___ __ __ __

4. ___ __ __ __ __ __ ___ __ __.

5. __ ___ __ __ __ __ __

6. __ __ ___ __ __ __ __ __ __ __

Teaching aims: Writing and spelling captions with the spelling <th>

Guidelines: Dictate the captions from the previous page to the student. Ask him/her to listen to the sounds in the words and say them as he/she writes them on the lines.

Book 8: Comprehension: Spot it!

1. Is the tramp up in the branches?	yes	no
2. Can you spot the belt?	yes	no
3. Can you spot the six gems?	yes	no
4. Can you spot Rat on the branch?	yes	no
5. Has the tramp got the gems in the bag?	yes	no
6. Is Zak sad?	yes	no
7. Is Zak catching the gems?	yes	no

Teaching guidelines:
This is a comprehension activity. Ask the student to look at the picture and answer the questions. He/she must then circle the words yes or no.

Book 8: Comprehension 2: Sequence the story

1.

2.

3.

4.

5.

6.

The tramp put the gems in a bag.

When Zak slept, a tramp crept up and got the belt.

The gems fell from the bag.

Rat nipped the tramp on his hand.

Rat ran up onto the branch and bit the bag.

Then the tramp sat on a branch and grinned at Zak.

Teaching guidelines:
Cut up the sentences above. Ask the student to read the sentences carefully and sequence them in the order of the story in Book 8, 'The Sixth Rock'. The student then sticks them in the numbered boxes in the correct order.
Words the student may need help with: put, the, gems, a when, his, onto

Book 8: Comprehension 3: Fill in the missing words

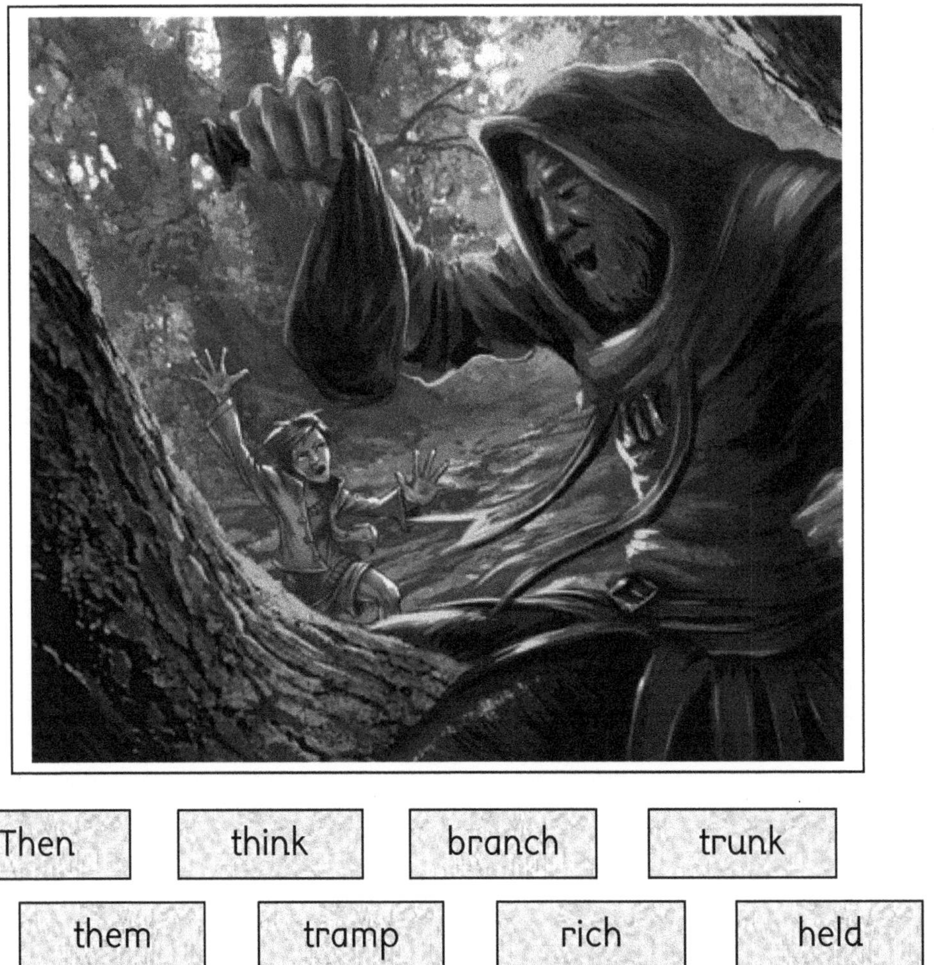

Then	think	branch	trunk
them	tramp	rich	held

The tramp sat on the _ _ _ _ __ and grinned.

He _ _ _ _ up the bag of gems.

"Give __ _ _ back!" yelled Zak.

"I __ _ _ _ not. I will sell them and get

_ _ __," said the _ _ _ _ _.

__ _ _ Rat ran up the tree _ _ _ _ _.

Teaching guidelines:
Ask the student to read the text and fill in the missing words. He/she should sound out the words as they write them on the lines. He/she can cross out the words in the boxes above as they use them in the text.

Book 8: Writing frame

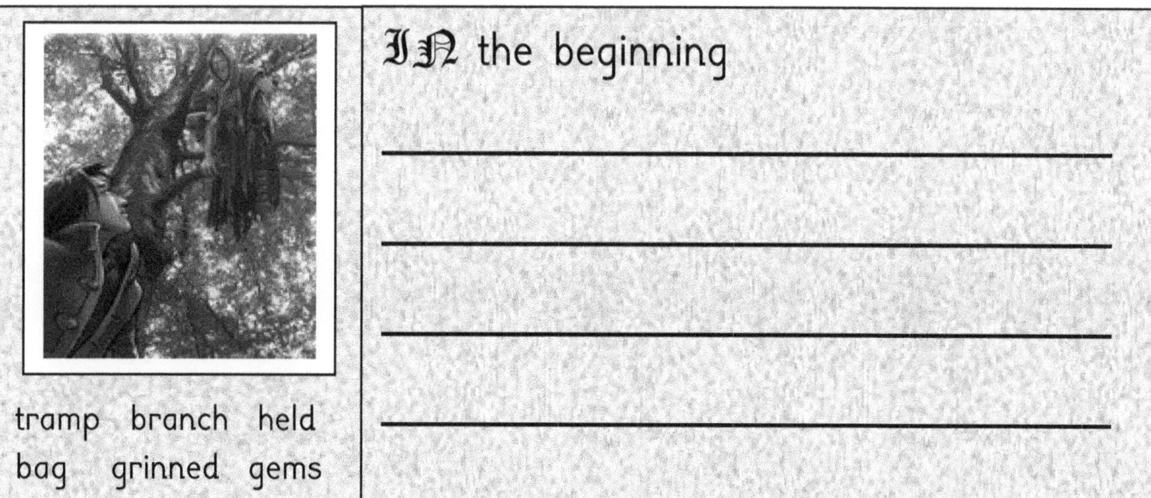

tramp branch held
bag grinned gems

IN the beginning

climbed tree trunk
thumped leg nipped

IN the middle

gems fell this
way that catch

IN the end

Teaching guidelines: Above is a writing frame to help the student to sequence the story. Some words are provided under the images to support spelling.

Book 8: Vocabulary

New words in Book 8:
flitted – flew or moved lightly and quickly
tramp – a person without a home or job who walks from place to place
grinned – smiled showing his teeth
spat – said it like he was spitting the words
frantic – distracted with fear
thumped – hit heavily

The moths flitted	thank Rat for this gem!"
The tramp was thin	next to the fire.
The tramp grinned	and had ragged clothes.
"I will get rich!"	and Zak was frantic.
The belt had gone	Finn with his leg.
The tramp thumped	at Zak and Finn.
Finn said, "We must	the tramp spat.

Teaching guidelines:
This activity includes new vocabulary introduced in Book 8, 'The Sixth Rock'. It encourages the student to think about the meaning of the new words and to use them to construct a complete sentence. Cut the sentences into strips and cut along the dotted line. Ask the student to match the two parts of the sentence so that they make sense. The student may need a reminder of what the words

Book 8: Punctuation activity

The tramp crept up to zak and finn he grabbed the belt the tramp was glad to get the belt

the tramp sat on a branch and grinned zak was frantic

rat ran up onto the branch he bit the bag the gems fell from the bag zak ran to catch them

Did you spot?

9 missing full stops

10 missing capital letters

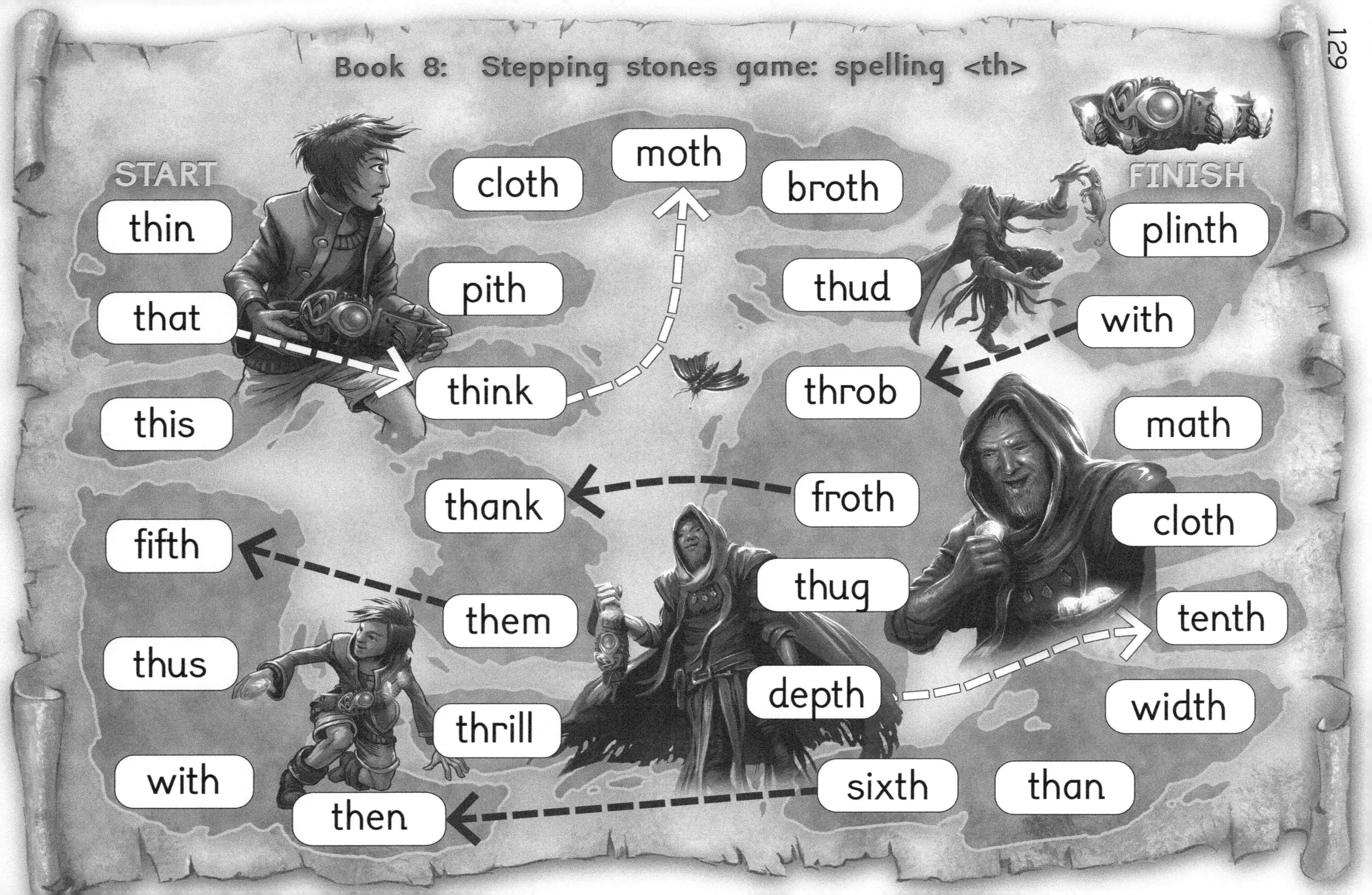
Book 8: Stepping stones game: spelling <th>
START
thin
that
this
fifth
thus
with
cloth
pith
think
thank
them
thrill
then
moth
broth
thud
throb
froth
thug
depth
sixth
than
FINISH
plinth
with
math
cloth
tenth
width

Book 9: Golem of the Rocks

Questions for discussion

Chapter 1

1. Zak said he was 'famished'. What did he mean? (p. 3)

Chapter 2

1. Why did the men hold their hands up to the sky? (p. 4)
2. What was stuck in the well? (p. 5)

Chapter 3

1. Why was the man in shock? (p. 6)
2. How did Finn find the well? (p. 7)

Chapter 4

1. How did Finn get the magic gem? (p. 9)
2. Why do you think the Golem stopped in his tracks? (p. 10)
3. What happened to the Golem when Finn held up the magic gem? (p. 11)
4. Why do you think the men went to see the stack of rocks? (p. 12)

Teaching guidelines:
These questions can be discussed after reading the text. They will help develop speaking and listening skills, comprehension and vocabulary.

Book 9: Word-building with <ck>

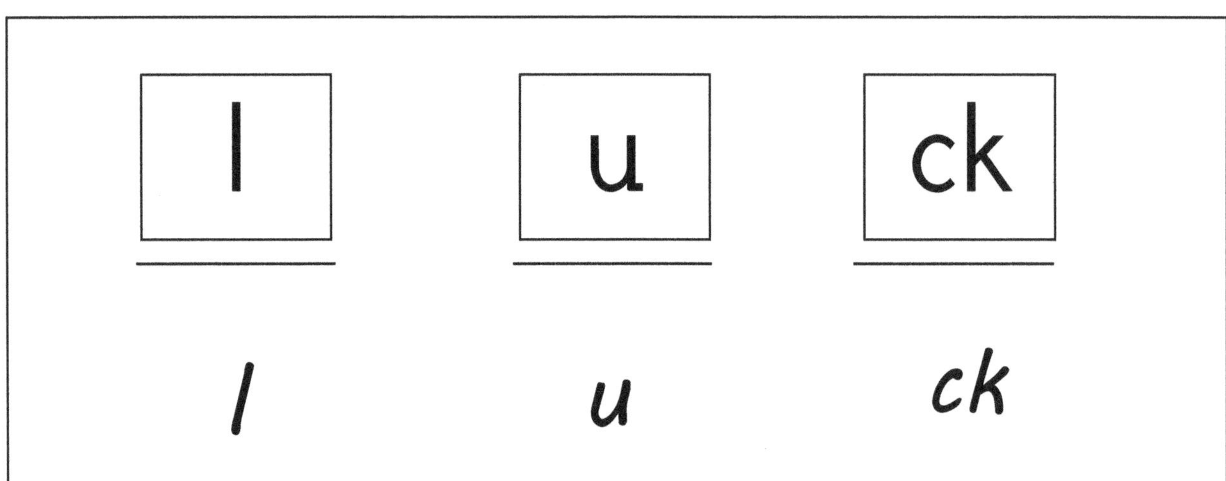

Teaching aims:

- learn the spelling alternative <ck> for the sound 'k'
- be able to segment and blend words with 'ck'

Teacher guidelines:
Use a white board on which three lines have been drawn. Make a card for the spelling <ck>. Add it to the cards with the letters of the alphabet from previous levels.

Teach word-building with the spelling <ck>
Select a word from the list below. Use only the letters needed to build that word and jumble them up. Ask the student to build that word by listening to the sounds in the word and segmenting all the sounds in the word, one at a time. The student then places each card on the appropriate line once he/she has segmented the word. Ask the student to read the word he/she has built. Ask the student to write the word under the lines, saying the sounds as he/she does. Draw more lines for longer words.

Teaching points:

1. Ask the student where the <ck> spelling appears in the word (end of word).
2. Ask the student if he/she knows other spellings for the sound 'k' (the letters c and k).

Word list for word-building, reading and spelling:
luck, sick, pack, back, peck, rock, suck, lick, kick, tick, lock, duck, chick, shock, muck, neck, check, shack, stick, slick, thick, trick, truck, black, smack, stack, pluck, track, click, flock, stuck

Book 9: Reading and spelling <ck>

luck	✓	__ __ ____	
check		____ __ ____	
rack		__ __ ____	
lock		__ __ ____	
pick		__ __ ____	
shack		____ __ ____	
trick		__ __ __ ____	
block		__ __ __ ____	
stuck		__ __ __ ____	

Teaching aims: Reading and spelling words with spelling <ck>

Teaching guidelines: Fold this sheet along the dotted line. Ask the student to read the words on the left and check off the words she/he has read correctly. Ask the student to turn over the sheet and dictate the words to the student. Ask the student to spell the words by segmenting and sounding out the sounds as she/he writes them on the lines. Ask the student to open the sheet and check off the words she/he has spelled correctly.

Book 9: 'ck'

Reading accuracy

luck
lick
lock

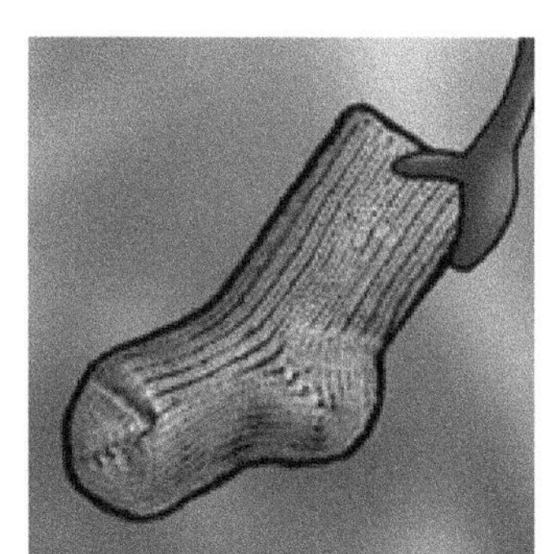

sock
suck
sick

block
rock
black

stack
stick
stuck

smack
truck
snack

clock
cluck
flock

Teaching aims: Reading accuracy

Teaching guidelines: Ask the student to read the words in each box and circle the word that matches the picture.

Book 9: <ck> nonsense words

Full circle game: playing with sounds

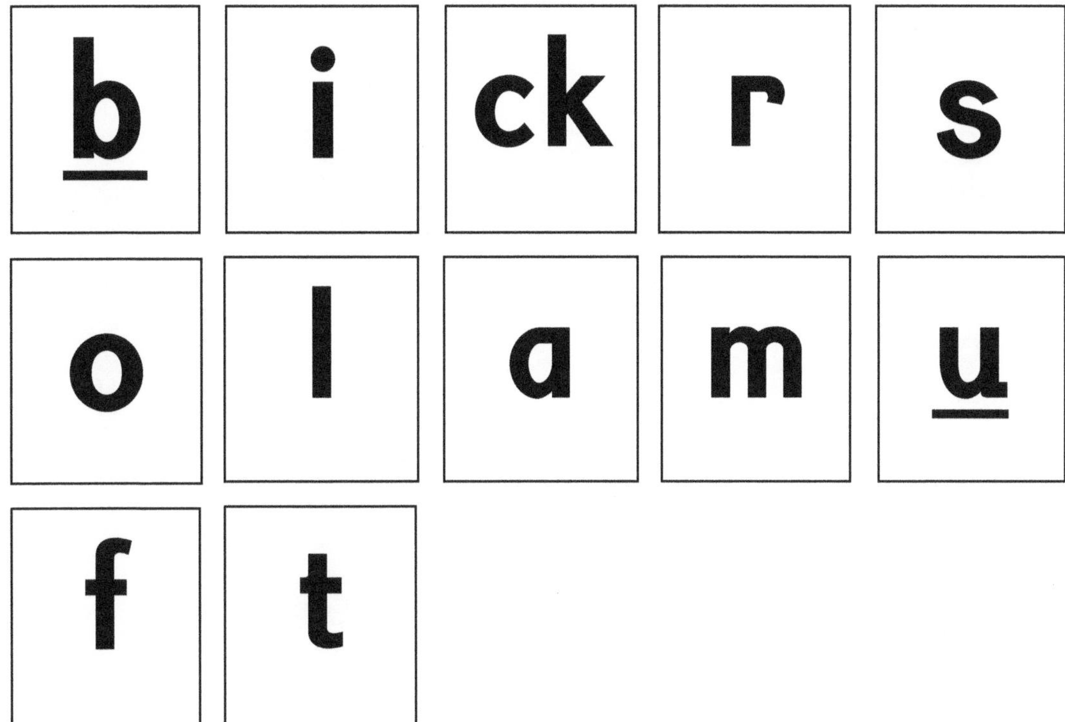

bick > brick > bricks > brocks > blocks > locks > lacks > lack > sack > smack > smick > smock > slock > flock > frock > fruck > sruck > struck > truck > trick > rick > bick

Teaching aims: Practice manipulating the sound 'k' with the spelling <ck> in nonsense words.

Teaching point: Manipulating sounds in nonsense words is a useful activity for older students as they are required to listen to sounds in words they have not seen before and therefore cannot rely on their visual memory. This develops their ability to segment sounds in words.

Teaching guidelines: Ask the student to build the word 'bick', using the cards above. Explain he/she will be building nonsense words. You are going to ask them to change one sound in the word to make a new word. He/she may need to add, take out or change a sound in the word. Ask the student to listen carefully to the new word and change it according to how it sounds. The word may be a real word or a nonsense word. Once the student has built the word ask him/her to read it. Complete the activity until the student has returned to the original word 'bick'.

Book 9: <ck>

Reading captions

1. thick, black ink

2. a big clock

3. a thin stick

4. a back pack

5. socks that match

6. a stack of bricks

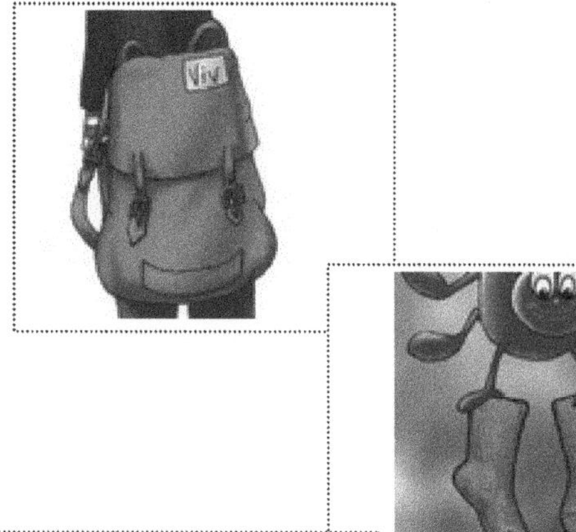

Teaching aims: Reading captions and comprehension

Teaching guidelines: Ask the student to read the captions and draw a line to the matching picture.

Teaching point: When reading high-frequency words, point to the grapheme the student does not yet know and sound it out for the student, e.g. with the word 'the', sound out 'th' and the shwa sound 'uh'.

Book 9: <ck>

Writing captions

1. ____ __ ____,   __ __ __ ____   __ __ __

2. __   __ __ __   __ __ __ ____

3. __   ____ __ __   __ __ __ ____

4. __   __ __ ____   __ __ ____

5. __ __ ____ __   ____ __ __   __ __ ______

6. __   __ __ __ ____   of   __ __ __ ____ __

Teaching aims: Writing and spelling captions with the spelling <ck>

Guidelines: Dictate the captions from the previous page to the student. Ask him/her to listen to the sounds in the words and say them as he/she writes them on the lines.

Book 9: Reading and spelling two-syllable words

Word	✓	Spelling	✓
back/rest	✓	_ _ _ _/_ _ _ _	
back/pack		_ _ _ _/_ _ _ _	
pad/lock		_ _ _/_ _ _ _	
un/stuck		_ _/_ _ _ _ _	
chop/stick		_ _ _ _/_ _ _ _ _	
pack/et		_ _ _ _/_ _	
crick/et		_ _ _ _ _/_ _	
jack/pot		_ _ _ _/_ _ _	
dip/stick		_ _ _/_ _ _ _ _	

Teaching aims: Reading and spelling words with the spelling <ck>

Teaching guidelines: Fold this sheet along the dotted line. Ask the student to read the words on the left and check off the words she/he has read correctly. Ask the student to turn over the sheet and dictate the words to the student. Ask the student to spell the words by segmenting and sounding out the sounds as she/he writes them on the lines. Ask the student to open the sheet and check off the words she/he has spelled correctly.

Book 9: Word-building with <qu>

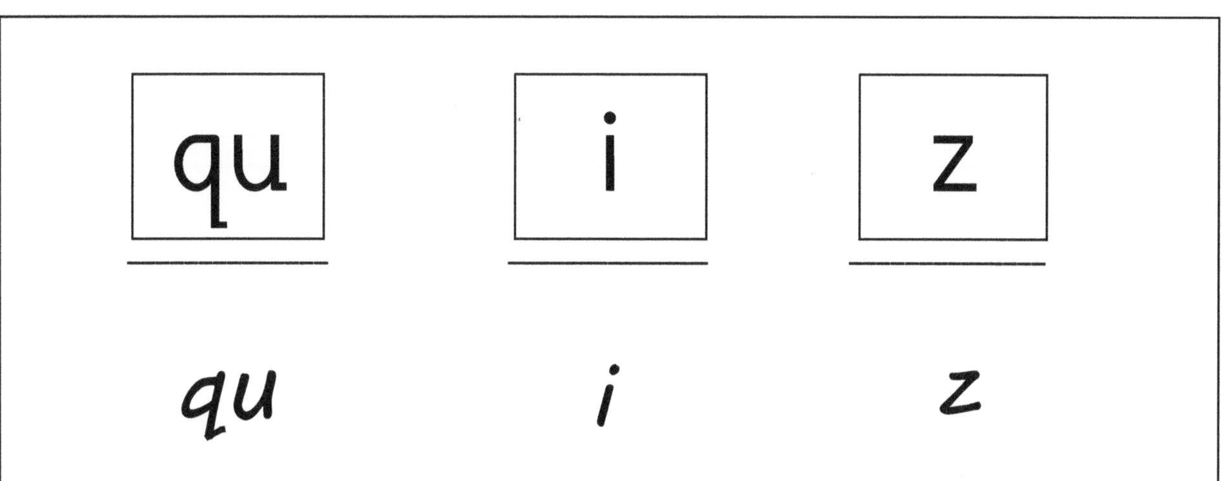

Note: The sound of the letter <q> is 'k' as in the word 'Iraq'. As this spelling is uncommon, the more common combination of the letters <qu> are taught as in the words: quick, queen etc. This common spelling represents two sounds – 'kw'.

Teaching aims:

- learn the sounds and spelling of <qu>
- segment and blend words with <qu>

Teacher guidelines:
Use a white board on which three lines have been drawn. Make a card for the spelling <qu>. Add it to the cards with the letters of the alphabet from previous levels.

Teach word-building with the spelling <qu>
Select a word from the list below. Use only the letters needed to build that word and jumble them up. Ask the student to build that word by listening to the sounds in the words and segmenting all the sounds in the words, one at a time. The student then places each card on the appropriate line once he/she has segmented the word. Ask the student to read the word he/she has built. Ask the student to write the word under the lines saying the sounds as he/she does. Draw more lines for longer words.

Word list for word-building, reading and spelling:
quit, quick, squish, quack, quest, quiff, quill, quiz, squid, quench, quilt, squint, squib

Book 9: Reading and spelling <qu>

Word	✓		Spelling	✓
quit	✓		___ ___ ___	
quack			___ ___ ___	
quiz			___ ___ ___	
quiff			___ ___ ___	
squish			___ ___ ___ ___	
quilt			___ ___ ___ ___	
quest			___ ___ ___ ___	
squid			___ ___ ___ ___	
quench			___ ___ ___ ___	

Teaching aims: Reading and spelling words with the spelling <qu>

Teaching guidelines: Fold this sheet along the dotted line. Ask the student to read the words on the left and check off the words she/he has read correctly. Ask the student to turn over the sheet and dictate the words to the student. Ask the student to spell the words by segmenting and sounding out the sounds as she/he writes them on the lines. Ask the student to open the sheet and check off the words she/he has spelled correctly.

Book 9: Comprehension: Spot it!

1. Can you spot the well?	yes	no
2. Is Finn checking the map?	yes	no
3. Can you spot the magic gem?	yes	no
4. Can you spot the Golem of the Rocks?	yes	no
5. Is the Golem attacking the village?	yes	no
6. Is Finn at the bottom of the well?	yes	no
7. Can you spot Zak and Rat?	yes	no

Teaching guidelines:
This is a comprehension activity. Ask the student to look at the picture and answer the questions. He/she must then circle the words yes or no.

Book 9: Comprehension 2: Sequence the story

1.
2.
3.
4.
5.
6.

The Golem wanted the gem and attacked the village.

The magic gem had got stuck at the bottom of the well.

A man begged Zak and Finn to help him.

The Golem of the Rocks collapsed into a stack of rocks.

Finn checked the map to get the magic gem.

Finn slid into the well and got the gem.

Teaching guidelines:
Cut up the sentences above. Ask the student to read the sentences carefully and sequence them in the order of the story in Book 9, 'Golem of the Rocks'. The student then sticks them in the numbered boxes in the correct order.
Words the student may need help with: the, wanted, gem, village, magic, of, to, into, a

Book 9: Comprehension 3: Fill in the missing words

back	slid	well	attacked
stack	stuck	rocks	smack

The Golem of the Rocks _ ___ _ ___ ___ the village. The magic gem was _ _ _ ___ at the bottom of the _ _ ___ and he wanted it. Finn _ _ _ _ into the well. He landed on his _ _ ___ with a _ _ _ ___! Finn held up the gem. It glinted. The Golem collapsed into a _ _ _ ___ of _ _ ___ _.

Teaching guidelines:
Ask the student to read the text and fill in the missing words. He/she should sound out the words as they write them on the lines. He/she can cross out the words in the boxes above as they use them in the text.

Book 9: Writing frame

Golem rocks wants
stuck bottom well

IN the beginning

____

____

____

____

slid into fast
smack hit back

IN the middle

____

____

____

____

gem glinted began
crack blocks fell

IN the end

____

____

____

____

Teaching guidelines: Above is a writing frame to help the student to sequence the story. Some words are provided under the images to support spelling.

Book 9: Vocabulary

New words in Book 9:

track – a path made by people or animals
jabbed – poked roughly
famished – extremely hungry
band of men – an organized group of people
flocked – gathered into a crowd
stack – a pile

Finn and Zak ran	the sky.
Big, thin rocks jabbed	so he got a snack.
Zak was famished	see the stack of rocks.
Zak saw a band of men	and fell on his back.
The men flocked to	on the track.
A stack of rocks is rocks	with their hands held up.
Finn slid into the well	on top of one another.

Teaching guidelines:
This activity includes new vocabulary introduced in Book 9, 'Golem of the Rocks'. It encourages the student to think about the meaning of the new words and to use them to construct a complete sentence. Cut the sentences into strips and cut along the dotted line. Ask the student to match the two parts of the sentence so that they make sense. The student may need a reminder of what the words mean.

Book 9: Punctuation activity

Zak and finn went along a track they met a band of men the men asked for their help

finn slid into the well he picked up the gem at the bottom this stopped the golem in his tracks

the golem collapsed into a stack of rocks the men went to see it

Did you spot?

8 missing full stops

10 missing capital letters

Book 9: Stepping stones game: spelling <ck> and <qu>

START

luck

sick

pack

quench

peck

rock

shock

chick

quilt

lock

kick

quest

liquid

squint

quick

check

shack

stick

thick

quiz

truck

black

FINISH

stuck

click

squid

pluck

quack

smack

This game is for 1–4 players. Play with counters and die. This sheet may be photocopied by the purchaser.

Book 10: Dung!

Questions for discussion

Chapter 1

1. Finn sang at the 'top of his lungs'. What does that mean? (p. 1)
2. Why did Zak not sing with Finn? (p. 2)
3. What is it like on the grasslands? (p. 3)

Chapter 2

1. Where did the smell come from? (p. 5)
2. What was the dung beetle doing? (p. 5)

Chapter 3

1. How did Zak try to get the gem from the ball of dung? (p. 7)
2. Why was Rat in danger? (p. 8)

Chapter 4

1. How did Zak rescue Rat? (p. 11)
2. What did the magic gem do in the end? (p. 12)

Teaching guidelines:
These questions can be discussed after reading the text. They will help develop speaking and listening skills, comprehension and vocabulary.

Book 10: Word-building with 'ng'

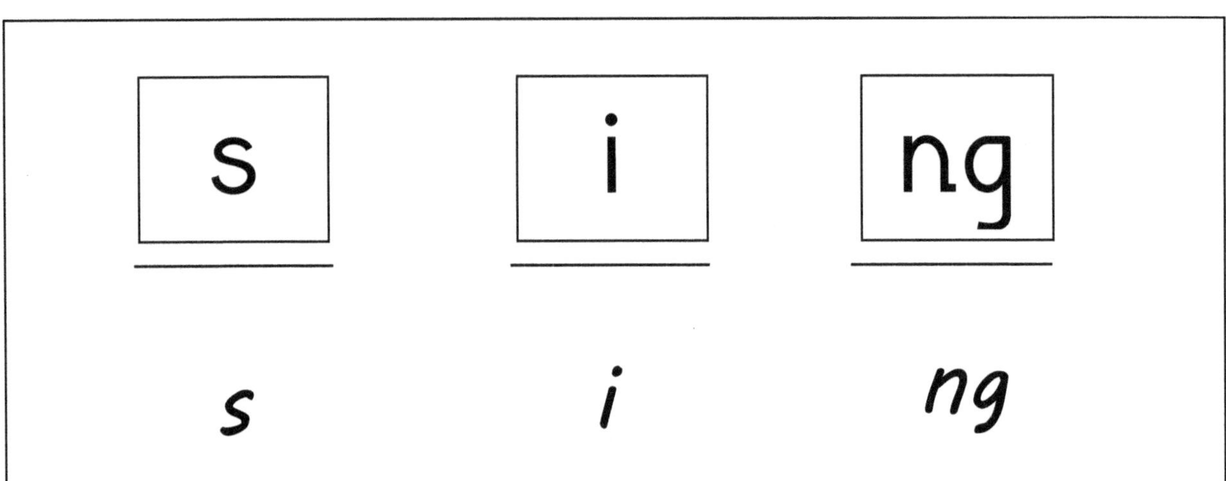

Teaching aims:

- learn the sound 'ng' and the corresponding spelling <ng>
- segment and blend words with 'ng'

Teacher guidelines:

Use a white board on which three lines have been drawn. Make a card for the spelling <ng>. Add it to the cards with the letters of the alphabet from previous levels.

Teach word-building with the spelling <ng>

Select a word from the list below. Use only the letters needed to build that word and jumble them up. Ask the student to build that word by listening to the sounds in the word and segmenting all the sounds in the word, one at a time. The student then places each card on the appropriate line once he/she has segmented the word. Ask the student to read the word he/she has built. Ask the student to write the word under the lines, saying the sounds as he/she does. Draw more lines for longer words.

Word list for word-building, reading and spelling:

sing, fang, long, ring, bang, pang, song, gong, king, lung, thing, gang, hang, dung, rang, wing, sling, bring, sting, cling, slang, swing, fling, clang, stung, strong, prong, twang, string

Book 10: Reading and spelling 'ng'

Word	✓	Spelling	✓
sing	✓	___ ___ _____	
bang		___ ___ _____	
long		___ ___ _____	
hung		___ ___ _____	
wing		___ ___ _____	
slang		___ ___ ___ _____	
bring		___ ___ ___ _____	
sting		___ ___ ___ _____	
strong		___ ___ ___ ___ _____	

Teaching aims: Reading and spelling words with the sound 'ng'

Teaching guidelines: Fold this sheet along the dotted line. Ask the student to read the words on the left and check off the words she/he has read correctly. Ask the student to turn over the sheet and dictate the words to the student. Ask the student to spell the words by segmenting and sounding out the sounds as she/he writes them on the lines. Ask the student to open the sheet and check off the words she/he has spelled correctly.

Book 10: 'ng'

Reading accuracy

 ring bring string	 sting sing swing	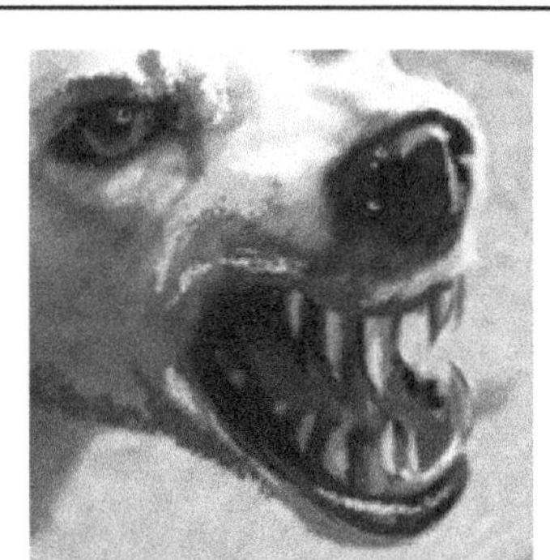 gang fang slang
 prong gong strong	 sting cling fling	 hang twang string

Teaching aims: Reading accuracy

Teaching guidelines: Ask the student to read the words in each box and circle the word that matches the picture.

Book 10: 'ng' nonsense words

Full circle game: playing with sounds

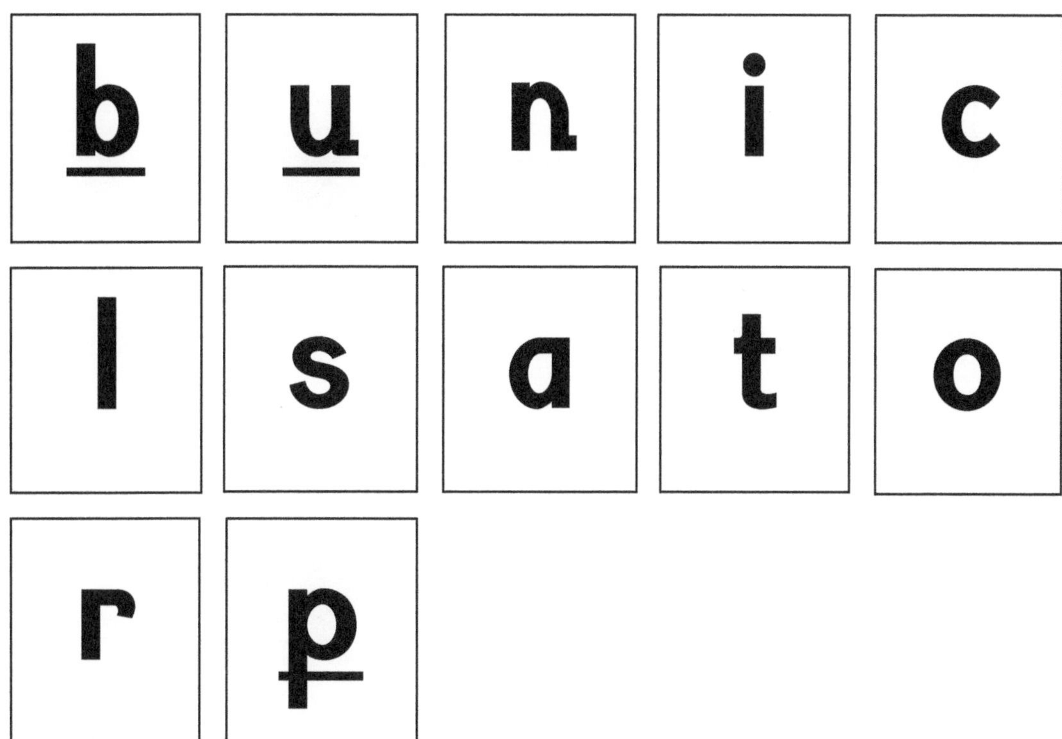

bung > bing > bling > pling > plings > plangs > plang > slang > stang > sting > stong > strong > string > strung > trung > rung > bung

Teaching aims: Practice manipulating the sound 'ng' in nonsense words.

Teaching point: Manipulating sounds in nonsense words is a useful activity for older students as they are required to listen to sounds in words they have not seen before and therefore cannot rely on their visual memory. This develops their ability to segment sounds in words.

Teaching guidelines: Ask the student to build the word 'bung', using the cards above. Explain he/she will be building nonsense words. You are going to ask them to change one sound in the word to make a new word. He/she may need to add, take out or change a sound in the word. Ask the student to listen carefully to the new word and change it according to how it sounds. The word may be a real word or a nonsense word. Once the student has built the word, ask him/her to read it. Complete the activity until the student has returned to the original word 'bung'.

Book 10: 'ng'

Reading captions

1. a bad sting

2. a strong man

3. a long track

4. fangs of a dog

5. Bang the gong.

6. a long string

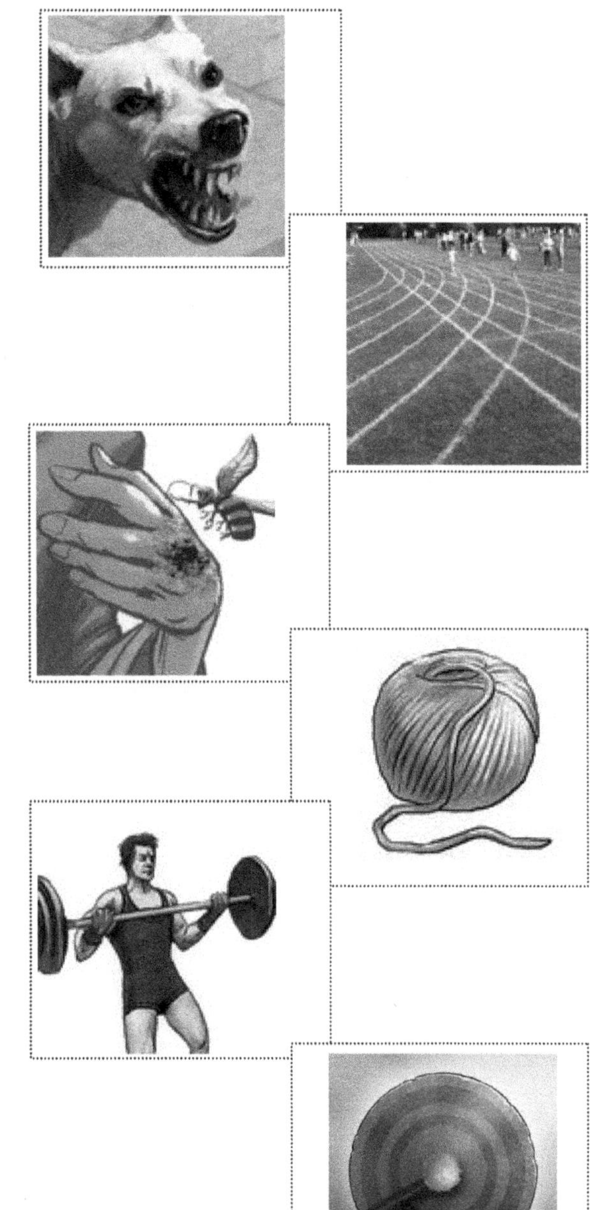

Teaching aims: Reading captions and comprehension

Teaching guidelines: Ask the student to read the captions and draw a line to the matching picture.

Teaching point: When reading high-frequency words, point to the grapheme the student does not yet know and sound it out for the student, e.g. with the word 'the', sound out 'th' and the shwa sound 'uh'.

Book 10: 'ng'

Writing captions

1. __   __ __ __   __ __ __ ____

2. __   __ __ __ __ ____   __ __ __

3. __   __ __ ____   __ __ __ ____

4. __ __ ____ __   of   __   __ __ __

5. __ __ ____   the   __ __ ____.

6. __   __ __ ____   __ __ __ __ ____

Teaching aims: Writing and spelling captions with the spelling 'ng'

Guidelines: Dictate the captions from the previous page to the student. Ask him/her to listen to the sounds in the words and say them as he/she writes them on the lines.

Book 10: Reading and spelling two-syllable words

sing/song	✓	_ _ __/_ _ __	
ob/long		_ _/_ _ __	
a/long		_/_ _ __	
be/long		_ _/_ _ __	
king/dom		_ _ __/_ _ _	
think/ing		__ _ _ _/_ __	
match/ing		_ _ ___/_ __	
rush/ing		_ _ __/_ __	
stick/ing		_ _ _ __/_ __	

Teaching aims: Reading and spelling words with 'ng'

Teaching guidelines: Fold this sheet along the dotted line. Ask the student to read the words on the left and check off the words she/he has read correctly. Ask the student to turn over the sheet and dictate the words to the student. Ask the student to spell the words by segmenting and sounding out the sounds as she/he writes them on the lines. Ask the student to open the sheet and check off the words she/he has spelled correctly.

Book 10: Comprehension: Spot it!

1. Can you spot the dung beetle?	yes	no
2. Can you spot the magic gem?	yes	no
3. Is Finn standing on the ball of dung?	yes	no
4. Is Rat clinging onto the ball of dung?	yes	no
5. Is Zak holding onto the ball of dung?	yes	no
6. Can you spot the rocks jabbing the sky?	yes	no
7. Is the dung beetle rolling the ball of dung?	yes	no

Teaching guidelines:
This is a comprehension activity. Ask the student to look at the picture and answer the questions. He/she must then circle the words yes or no.

Book 10: Comprehension 2: Sequence the story

1.
2.
3.
4.
5.
6.

Zak got his sling shot, but the gem was stuck.

The dung beetle shrank and buzzed off.

The magic gem was stuck in the ball of dung.

Finn yanked the gem from the ball of dung.

The lads saw a dung beetle rolling a ball of dung.

Rat ran onto the ball, but he almost got crushed.

Teaching guidelines:
Cut up the sentences above. Ask the student to read the sentences carefully and sequence them in the order of the story in Book 10, 'Dung!'.
Words the student may need help with: his, the, gem, was, beetle, magic, ball, of, saw, a, rolling, onto, almost

Book 10: Comprehension 3: Fill in the missing words

Twang	cling	strength	onto
magic	stuck	dung	rock

The _ _ _ _ _ gem was hidden in the ball of _ _ __. Zak got his sling shot. _ _ _ __! Ping! The _ _ __ hit the dung, but the gem was _ _ _ __! Rat ran _ _ _ _ the ball of dung. The dung beetle rolled it. Rat had to _ _ _ __ on with all his _ _ _ _ __ __.

Teaching guidelines:
Ask the student to read the text and fill in the missing words. He/she should sound out the words as they write them on the lines. He/she can cross out the words in the boxes above as they use them in the text.

Book 10: Writing frame

black thing ball
dung beetle smelled

IN the beginning

____

____

____

____

jumped clung all
strength their hands

IN the middle

____

____

____

____

little beetle stretched
wings buzzed off

IN the end

____

____

____

____

Teaching guidelines: Above is a writing frame to help the student to sequence the story. Some words are provided under the images to support spelling.

Book 10: Vocabulary

New words in Book 10:
dung – waste products from large animals
top of his lungs – in his loudest voice
longed – wanted it very much
snapped – said it quickly and angrily
grasslands – flat land which is mostly grass
stench – a very unpleasant smell
livid – very angry

Zak missed his Grandpa.	It was livid.
Zap was sad and he	at the top of his lungs.
Grassland is land that	He longed for him.
A stench is a very	snapped at Finn.
Finn was happy and sang	of dung. It smelled bad.
The beetle was angry.	is flat with lots of grass.
Zak and Finn saw a ball	bad smell.

Teaching guidelines:
This activity includes new vocabulary introduced in Book 10, 'Dung!'. It encourages the student to think about the meaning of the new words and to use them to construct a complete sentence. Cut the sentences into strips and cut along the dotted line. Ask the student to match the two parts of the sentence so that they make sense. The student may need a reminder of what the words mean.

Book 10: Punctuation activity

The lads saw a big black thing it
was a black dung beetle it was
rolling a ball of dung

the magic gem was stuck in the ball
of dung zak got his sling shot, but the
gem was stuck

rat ran onto the dung the beetle
rolled the ball rat almost got crushed

Did you spot?

8 missing full stops

7 missing capital letters

Book 10: Stepping stones game: 'ng'

START

sing
fang
king
long
ring
bang

hang
gang
thing
gong
song
pang
lung

dung
rang
wing
sling
bring
sting
cling
slang
swing

FINISH

string
prong
strong
stung
clang
fling

This game is for 1–4 players. Play with counters and die. This sheet may be photocopied by the purchaser.

Book 11: The Spitting Pot

Questions for discussion

Chapter 1

1. Finn inspected the map. What does that mean? (p. 1)
2. Why did the lads feel like the rocks were mocking them? (p. 2)

Chapter 2

1. Why do you think there was a stench of rotting flesh coming from the pot? (p. 4)
2. Finn threw a rock into the pot. Why do you think it melted? (p. 6)

Chapter 3

1. Why did Finn step away from the spitting pot? (p. 8)
2. How did Zak's hatchet fall from his hand? (p. 9)

Chapter 4

1. What happened to Rat? (p. 10)
2. How did Zak rescue Rat? (pp. 11, 12)

Teaching guidelines:
These questions can be discussed after reading the text. They will help develop speaking and listening skills, comprehension and vocabulary.

Book 11: Word-building with 'wh'

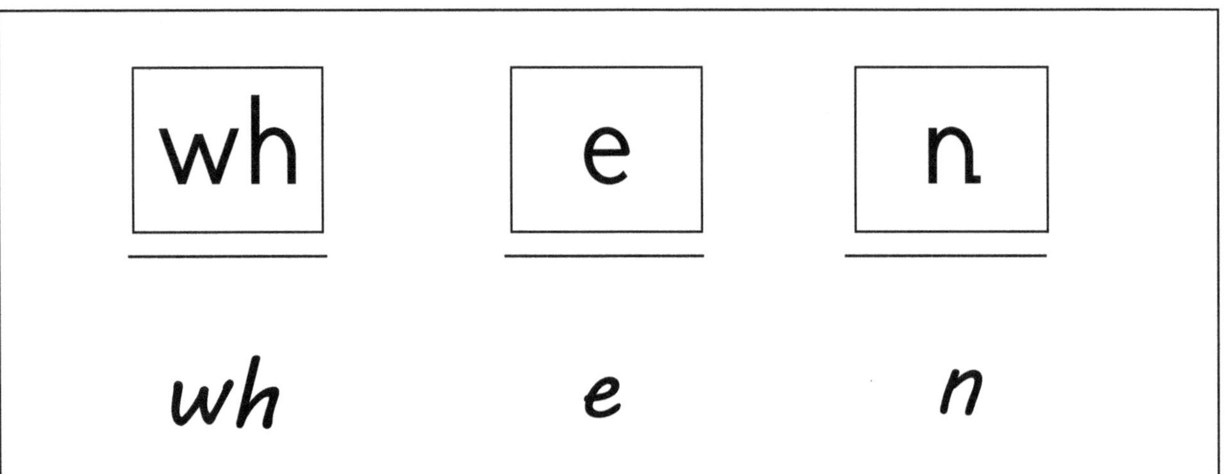

Teaching aims:

- learn the alternative spelling <wh> for the sound 'w'
- segment and blend words with <wh>

Teacher guidelines:

Use a white board on which three lines have been drawn. Make a card for the spelling <wh>. Add it to the cards with the letters of the alphabet from previous levels.

Teach word-building with the spelling <wh>

Select a word from the list below. Use only the letters needed to build that word and jumble them up. Ask the student to build that word by listening to the sounds in the word and segmenting all the sounds in the word, one at a time. The student then places each card on the appropriate line once he/she has segmented the word. Ask the student to read the word he/she has built. Ask the student to write the word under the lines, saying the sounds as he/she does. Draw more lines for longer words.

Word list for word-building, reading and spelling:

when, which, whip, whack, whim, whisk, whiff, wham, whet, whiz

Book 11: Reading and spelling <wh>

when	✓	___ __ __	
which		___ __ ___	
whip		___ __ __	
whack		___ __ ___	
whim		___ __ __	
whiff		___ __ ___	
whiz		___ __ __	
whisk		___ __ __ __	
wham		___ __ __	

Teaching aims: Reading and spelling words with the spelling <wh>

Teaching guidelines: Fold this sheet along the dotted line. Ask the student to read the words on the left and check off the words she/he has read correctly. Ask the student to turn over the sheet and dictate the words to the student. Ask the student to spell the words by segmenting and sounding out the sounds as she/he writes them on the lines. Ask the student to open the sheet and check off the words she/he has spelled correctly.

Book 11: Reading and spelling two-syllable words

whisking	✓	*whisk / ing*	
whamming		/	
whipping		/	
whizzing		/	
whelping		/	
whacking		/	
whittling		/	
whiffing		/	
whetting		/	

Teaching aims: Reading and spelling words with <wh> and the suffix -ing

Teaching guidelines: **Teaching guidelines**: This activity allows the teacher to use his/her preferable method of splitting words into syllables. For different approaches to splitting syllables see page 3. Fold this sheet along the dotted line. Ask the student to read the words on the left and check off the words she/he has read correctly. Ask the student to turn over the sheet and dictate the words to the student. Ask the student to split the words into two syllables and to write a syllable on each side of the slash. Ask the student to sound out the syllables as she/he writes them. Ask the student to open the sheet and check off the words she/he has spelled correctly.

Book 11: Splitting two syllable-words with -ing

sitting		
betting		
cutting		
spotting		
linking		
handing		
sending		
bonding		
pumping		

Teaching aims: Learning to split two syllable words with the suffix -ing.

Teaching guidelines: This activity allows the teacher to use his/her own approach to splitting syllables. To see the different approaches see page 3 of this workbook. Teachers who use the spelling-rules approach may wish to teach their students the 'doubling rule' at this point.

Book 11: Reading and spelling with suffix –ing

lifting	✓	/	
jumping		/	
helping		/	
thinking		/	
sitting		/	
shopping		/	
bringing		/	
stopping		/	
dripping		/	

Teaching aims: Reading and spelling words with the suffix –ing

Teaching guidelines: This activity allows the teacher to use his/her preferable method of splitting words into syllables. For different approaches to splitting syllables see page 3. Fold this sheet along the dotted line. Ask the student to read the words on the left and check off the words she/he has read correctly. Ask the student to turn over the sheet and dictate the words to the student. Ask the student to split the words into two syllables and to write a syllable on each side of the slash. Ask the student to sound out the syllables as she/he writes them. Ask the student to open the sheet and check off the words she/he has spelled correctly.

Book 11: –ing

Reading captions

1. jumping off

2. chopping logs

3. hanging on

4. sitting on a mat

5. thinking a lot

6. dripping wet

Teaching aims: Reading captions and comprehension

Teaching guidelines: Ask the student to read the captions and draw a line to the matching picture.

Teaching point: When reading high-frequency words, point to the grapheme the student does not yet know and sound it out for the student, e.g. with the word 'the', sound out 'th' and the shwa sound 'uh'.

Book 11: Comprehension: Spot it!

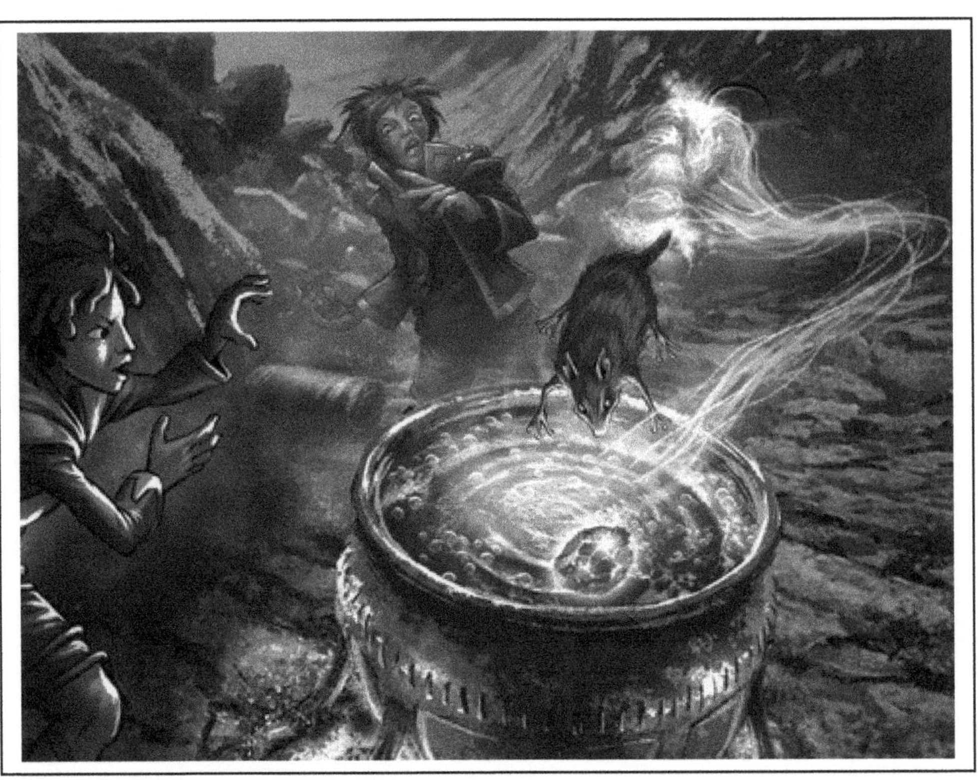

1. Can you spot the spitting pot?	yes	no
2. Can you spot the magic gem?	yes	no
3. Can you spot the acid liquid?	yes	no
4. Is Rat dangling on top of the pot?	yes	no
5. Is Zak holding a rug?	yes	no
6. Is the spitting pot tipping?	yes	no
7. Is the spitting pot bubbling?	yes	no

Teaching guidelines:
This is a comprehension activity. Ask the student to look at the picture and answer the questions. He/she must then circle the words yes or no.

Book 11: Comprehension 2: Sequence the story

1.

2.

3.

4.

5.

6.

The evil spirit dangled Rat inches from the liquid acid.

The magic gem was in the bubbling pot.

Pink liquid acid jumped out at him.

Zak kicked the pot, tipping the evil spirit onto the rocks.

The evil spirit jumped from the pot, landing next to Finn.

Finn ran up to the spitting pot.

Teaching guidelines:
Cut up the sentences above. Ask the student to read the sentences carefully and sequence them in the order of the story in Book 11, 'The Spitting Pot'. The student then sticks then in the numbered boxes in the correct order.
Words the student may need help with: The, evil, dangled, acid, magic, gem, was, out, onto,

Book 11: Comprehension 3: Fill in the missing words

jumped	him	evil	spitting
acid	liquid	melting	stepping

Suddenly, an ____________ spirit shot up and began ____________ from the pot. Finn ____________ back. The stinking ____________ landed next to ____________, sizzling and ____________ the rocks. "It is ____________ in the pot!" yelled Finn, ____________ back.

Teaching guidelines:
Ask the student to read the text and fill in the missing words. He/she can cross out the words in the boxes above as they use them in the text.

Book 11: Writing frame

IN the beginning

spitting pot bubbling
hissing pink liquid

IN the middle

sniffing spirit whisked
dangling inches acid

IN the end

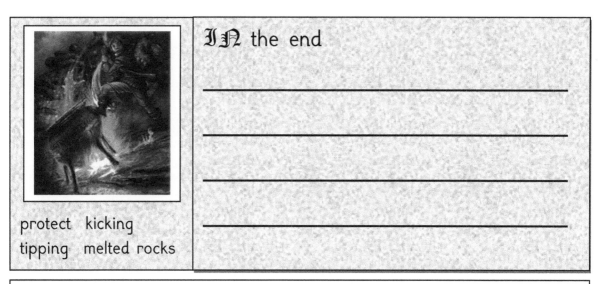

protect kicking
tipping melted rocks

Teaching guidelines: Above is a writing frame to help the student to sequence the story. Some words are provided under the images to support spelling.

Book 11: Vocabulary

New words in Book 11:
inspecting – looking at and checking something carefully
mocking – making fun of someone
rotting flesh – meat that has gone bad
chucked – threw
sizzling – making a hissing sound like frying fat
acid – a substance that can eat away at other materials
dangling – hanging or swinging loosely

Zak was inspecting the	of rotting flesh.
The lads felt that the rocks	map to find the well.
The spitting pot smelled	from the bubbling pot.
Finn chucked a rock	acid at Finn.
Rat's tail was sizzling from	in the pot and it melted.
The evil spirit spat	the grip of the spirit.
Rat was dangling inches	were mocking them.

Teaching guidelines:
This activity includes new vocabulary introduced in Book 11, 'The Spitting Pot'. It encourages the student to think about the meaning of the new words and to use them to construct a complete sentence. Cut the sentences into strips and cut along the dotted line. Ask the student to match the two parts of the sentence so that they make sense. The student may need a reminder of what the words mean.

Book 11: Punctuation activity

The evil spirit grabbed rat it held him inches from the spitting pot the pot was sizzling and hissing

zak held up the rug to protect himself he kicked the pot with his leg the pot tipped and spilled the pink liquid melted into the rocks little rat's tail was sizzling

Did you spot?

8 missing full stops

9 missing capital letters

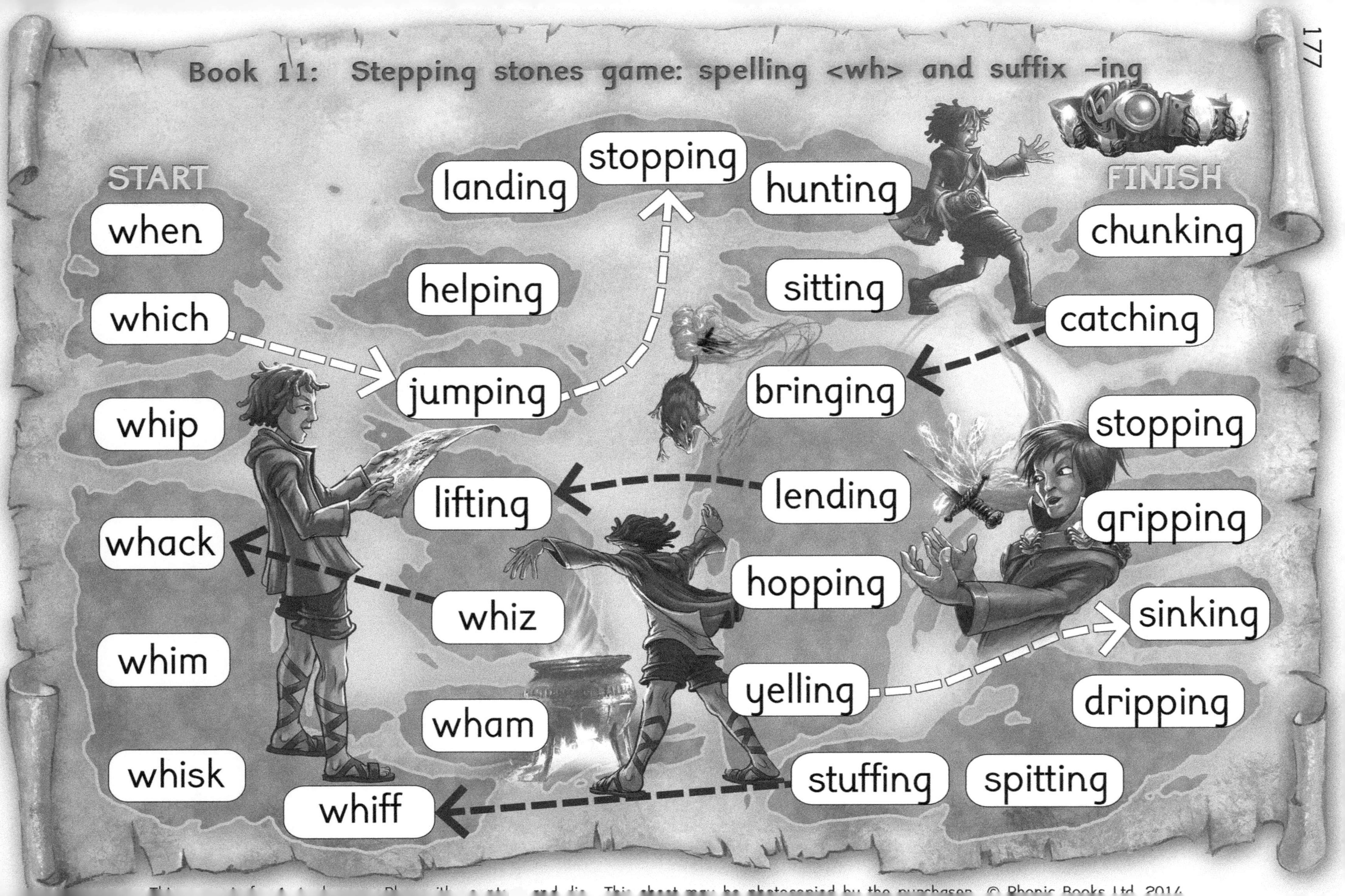
Book 11: Stepping stones game: spelling <wh> and suffix –ing
START
FINISH
when
which
whip
whack
whim
whisk
landing
helping
jumping
lifting
whiz
wham
whiff
stopping
hunting
sitting
bringing
lending
hopping
yelling
stuffing
chunking
catching
stopping
gripping
sinking
dripping
spitting

Book 12: The Simple Plot

Questions for discussion

Chapter 1

1. Why was Zak baffled? (p. 1)
2. Where did the magic belt drag them back to? (p. 2)

Chapter 2

1. Who had the last magic gem? (p. 3)
2. Why did the wizard make Grandpa sick? (p. 5)
3. The wizard told Rat to "finish the job!" What did he mean? (p. 6)

Chapter 3

1. Why was Rat puzzled? (p. 8)
2. Why did Rat go for the wizard? (p. 9)

Chapter 4

1. What do you think was Zak's wish? (pp. 10, 11)
2. Where does Finn go in the wagon? (p. 12)
3. Why did Finn tell Zak to "Look out for men in red hats"? (p. 12)

Teaching guidelines:
These questions can be discussed after reading the text. They will help develop speaking and listening skills, comprehension and vocabulary.

Book 12: Splitting two-syllable words with <le> ending

apple		
pebble		
muddle		
little		
simple		
handle		
temple		
bundle		
bramble		

Teaching aims: Learning to split two syllable words with the suffix –ing.

Teaching guidelines: This activity allows the teacher to use his/her own approach to splitting syllables. To see the different approaches see page 3 of this workbook. Teachers who use the spelling-rules approach may wish to teach their students the 'doubling rule' at this point.

Book 12: Reading and spelling words ending with <le>

Word	✓	Spelling	✓
apple	✓	/	
puddle		/	
middle		/	
bottle		/	
little		/	
gobble		/	
simple		/	
handle		/	
single		/	

Teaching aims: Reading and spelling words ending with the spelling <le>

Teaching guidelines: This activity allows the teacher to use his/her preferable method of splitting words into syllables. For different approaches to splitting syllables see page 3. Fold this sheet along the dotted line. Ask the student to read the words on the left and check off the words she/he has read correctly. Ask the student to turn over the sheet and dictate the words to the student. Ask the student to split the words into two syllables and to write a syllable on each side of the slash. Ask the student to sound out the syllables as she/he writes them. Ask the student to open the sheet and check off the words she/he has spelled correctly.

Book 12: <le>

Reading captions

1. dripping candle

2. a simple sum

3. a single sock

4. a little puddle

5. Fling the pebble.

6. in the middle

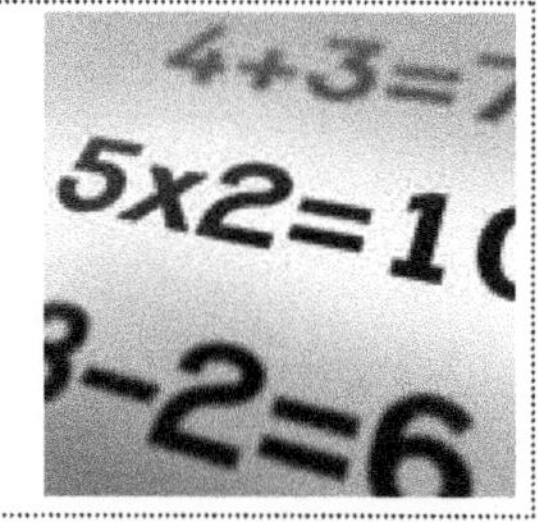

Teaching aims: Reading captions and comprehension

Teaching guidelines: Ask the student to read the captions and draw a line to the matching picture.

Teaching point: When reading high-frequency words, point to the grapheme the student does not yet know and sound it out for the student, e.g. with the word 'the', sound out 'th' and the shwa sound 'uh'.

Book 12: Comprehension: Spot it!

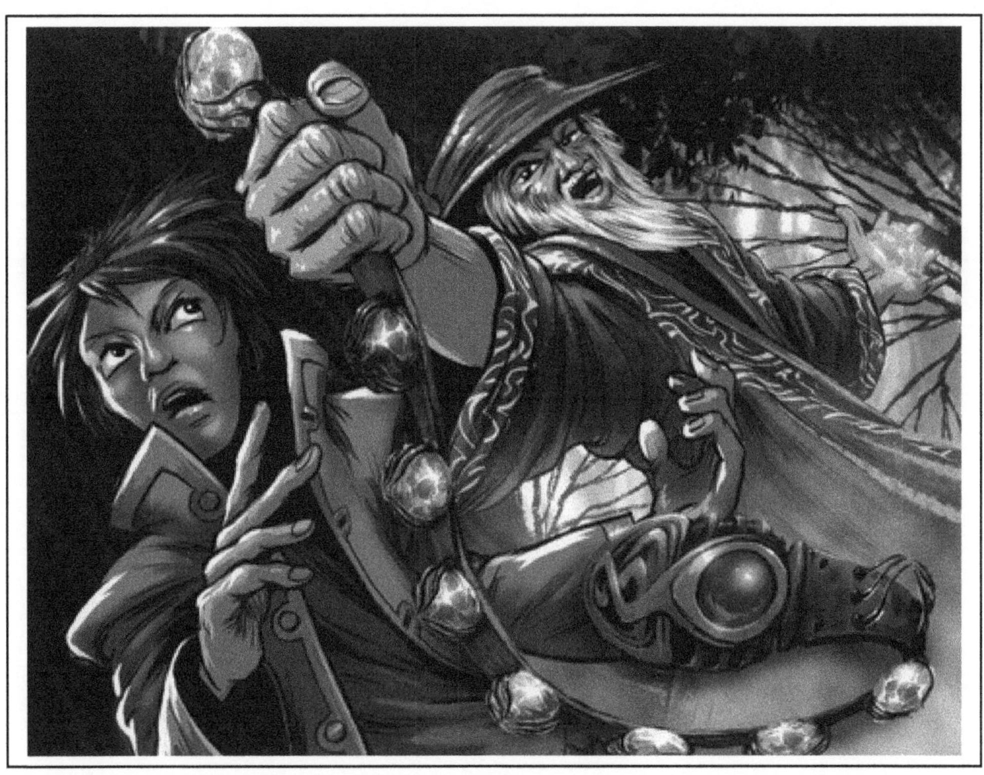

1. Can you spot the bad wizard?	yes	no
2. Is the wizard grabbing the belt?	yes	no
3. Can you spot the missing gem?	yes	no
4. Is the tenth gem fixed to the belt?	yes	no
5. Is Finn tackling the wizard?	yes	no
6. Is the wizard yelling?	yes	no
7. Is Zak grinning?	yes	no

Teaching guidelines:
This is a comprehension activity. Ask the student to look at the picture and answer the questions. He/she must then circle the words yes or no.

Book 12: Comprehension 2: Sequence the story

1.

2.

3.

4.

5.

6.

The evil wizard told Rat to attack the lads.

The evil wizard grabbed the belt from Zak.

Grandpa sat up in bed, looking well.

Zak made a wish and the magic belt became a goblet.

The magic belt dragged Zak and Finn back to the forest.

Rat went for the wizard. The wizard stumbled off.

Teaching guidelines:
Cut up the sentences above. Ask the student to read the sentences carefully and sequence them in the order of the story in Book 12, 'The Simple Plot'.
Words the student may need help with: the, evil, wizard, told, to, looking, made, a, magic, became, for

Book 12: Comprehension 3: Fill in the missing words

yelled	strong	job	massive
battle	ducked	rodent	wand

"Finish the ____________!" the evil wizard ____________ at Rat. The wizard tapped his ____________. Rat became a ____________ rat. He began to ____________ with Finn. Finn tackled the massive ____________. He struggled. Rat was as ____________ as an ox, but Finn ____________.

Teaching guidelines:
Ask the student to read the text and fill in the missing words. He/she should sound out the words as they write them on the lines. He/she can cross out the words in the boxes above as they use them in the text.

Book 12: Writing frame

dragged back forest
evil wizard grabbed

IN the beginning

____

____

____

____

attacked looked
puzzled wizard

IN the middle

____

____

____

____

wish magic Grandpa
goblet sipped well

IN the end

____

____

____

____

Teaching guidelines: Above is a writing frame to help the student to sequence the story. Some words are provided under the images to support spelling.

Book 12: Vocabulary

New words in Book 12:
baffled – puzzled
cackled – laughed in a shrill manner
rumbled – said in a deep way like thunder
mumbled – spoke softly and unclearly
ox – a male cow used for pulling carts
stumbled – lost balance or fell over something

Zak was baffled as the	in a horrid way.
The evil wizard cackled	wizard rumbled.
"Give me the belt!" the	belt dragged him back.
"Will you help Grandpa?"	into the forest.
The wizard tapped	an ox.
Rat was as strong as	his wand.
The wizard stumbled	Zak mumbled.

Teaching guidelines:
This activity includes new vocabulary introduced in Book 12, 'A Simple Plot'. It encourages the student to think about the meaning of the new words and to use them to construct a complete sentence. Cut the sentences into strips and cut along the dotted line. Ask the student to match the two parts of the sentence so that they make sense. The student may need a reminder of what the words mean.

Book 12: Punctuation activity

The wizard had made grandpa sick with a magic spell he had sent zak on the quest to get him the ten magic gems

the wizard told the rat to attack finn and zak the rat went for the wizard the wizard stumbled into the forest

Did you spot?

5 missing full stops

8 missing capital letters

Book 12: Stepping stones game: spelling <le>

START

apple

little

gamble

simple

FINISH

dangle

pebble

kettle

single

giggle

saddle

handle

fiddle

mumble

muffle

temple

gobble

grapple

mantle

puddle

stumble

muddle

candle

bramble

middle

gabble

settle

dimple

ramble

This game is for 1–4 players. Play with counters and die. This sheet may be photocopied by the purchaser.

The Magic Belt Series: Book review

What did you like about the series?

What was your favorite book in the series and why?

Who was your favorite character and why?

Would you recommend it to your friends? Why?